THE SICKNESS

ALBERTO BARRERA TYSZKA is a poet, novelist and journalist. Together with Cristina Marcano he wrote the bestselling and critically acclaimed *Hugo Chávez* (2007), the first biography of the Venezuelan president. *The Sickness* was the winner of the prestigious Herralde Prize in its original Spanish edition and is shortlisted for the 2011 *Independent* Foreign Fiction Prize. He has also co-scripted a film and written for *telenovelas*.

MARGARET JULL COSTA is the translator of many Portuguese, Spanish and Latin-American writers, amongst them José Saramago, Javier Marías, Bernardo Atxaga and Fernando Pessoa. She was won many awards, the most recent being the 2008 Oxford Weidenfeld Translation prize and the 2010 Premio Valle Inclán.

"A short, tersely written novel that distances and invades us at the same time. Powerful themes and powerful writing that do not let you off or let you down"
                                                            SUSAN HILL, *Lady*

"It is movingly described and all too believable. Tyszka's remarkable novel is poised and human ... Tyszka is a perceptive, original writer. He has brought an unusually sophisticated understanding to a wonderfully intense, little novel. No sentimentality, no polemic, just emotion at its most resonant"
                                                    EILEEN BATTERSBY, *Irish Times*

"*The Sickness* is a calmly paced novel unafraid to linger in scenes long enough to realize their potential, but never so long that they become tedious ... Tyszka can reduce his through-lines to something resembling the first principles of a systematic philosopher . . . *The Sickness* is refreshingly clean in its storytellin...character"
                                                    EY, *Times Literary Supplement*

"Alberto ... identity from a hypochondriac's p...sis"
                                                    BOYD TONKIN, *Independent*

"A small masterpiece . . . Many things are beautifully observed in this book . . . I assumed at first that the book was written by a doctor, that Alberto Barrera Tyszka was 'one of us', the highest compliment I could pay him"

THEODORE DALRYMPLE, *British Medical Journal*

"More than holds its own in terms of tone, character and storytelling. The philosophy within the story is well pitched, gentle and suggestive, and despite the sinister and sceptical undercurrents, does not preach, but questions belief by provoking opinion on topics around medicine, illness, pain and death"

RENÉE ROWLAND, *Skinny*

"A provocative, artfully wrought novel"

VIVIENNE NILAN, *Athens Plus*

"Part of this novel's beauty comes from its eloquent portrayal of how even the most prepared among us can be overwhelmed or ambushed by disaster . . . One can read this book as an investigation of a nation's psyche as it endures a sickness that leaves no-one untouched"

GUILLERMO PARRA, author of *Caracas Notebook*

"Written in direct and lyrical prose, *The Sickness* promises to place Tyszka at the front rank of new Latin American writers, and, in its poignant dissection of middle-class malaise and familial dynamics, establishes him with a claim to be the Venezuelan Ian McEwan"

Booktrust Translated Fiction

"A believable, sensitive meditation on love and loss . . . an engaging, readable exploration of death and dying . . . veering from the poignant to the comic and back again . . . Tyszka's great skill is to evoke an emotional response from a series of lightly sketched but nonetheless highly believable epiphanies"

VAL NOLAN, *Irish Examiner*

Alberto Barrera Tyszka

THE SICKNESS

Translated from the Spanish by
Margaret Jull Costa

MACLEHOSE PRESS
QUERCUS · LONDON

First published in Great Britain in 2010 by MacLehose Press
This paperback edition first published in 2011 by

MacLehose Press
an imprint of Quercus
21 Bloomsbury Square
London, WC1A 2NS

First published in Spanish as *La Enfermedad* by
Editorial Anagrama, Barcelona, 2006
Copyright © 2006 by Alberto Barrera Tyszka

English translation copyright © 2010 by Margaret Jull Costa

A CIP catalogue reference for this book is available
from the British Library

ISBN 978 1 84916 403 0

2 4 6 8 10 9 7 5 3 1

Typeset by in Albertina MT by
Libanus Press, Marlborough
Printed and bound in Great Britain
by Clays Ltd, St Ives plc

THE SICKNESS

I

"Are the results in yet?"

No sooner are the words out of his mouth than he regrets having spoken them. Andrés Miranda wishes he could catch the question in mid-air and send it back where it came from, hide it away again beneath a silence. But he can't, it's too late. Now all Andrés has is the chief radiologist's face, his lips a knot in the middle of his mouth, his dark eyes like two stains, as he offers Andrés a smile of strained sympathy and hands him a large brown envelope. The radiologist says nothing, but his very expression is a judgement: multiple lesions suggestive of a metastatic disease, for example. That, more or less, is what the knotted lips are saying. Medical people rarely use adjectives. They don't need to.

"Are the results of the C.T. scan in as well?"

The radiologist shakes his head and shifts his gaze to the corridor.

"I was told they were being sent direct to you."

Andrés feels strangely embarrassed, as if both of them were making a tremendous effort not to upset the fragile balance of the moment. He thanks his colleague and makes his way back to his office. No-one has told him as much, he hasn't even seen the X-rays, he hasn't been shown the results, and yet he knows that his father has cancer.

Why do we find it so hard to accept that life is pure chance? That is the question Miguel always asks before any operation. There they all are wearing green gowns, gloves and surgical

1

masks; the white light of the operating theatre seems to float on the cold air-conditioned air. And then Miguel picks up a scalpel, looks at Andrés and asks: "Why do we find it so hard to accept that life is pure chance?" Some of the nurses dislike this as a prelude to an operation. Perhaps they realise that it's not exactly a good way to start, almost a prior justification in case anything should go wrong. Andrés is sure this isn't so, for he knows Miguel well; they've been friends since they were students. There's no cynicism in that question. It seems, rather, an expression of self-compassion, a kindly prayer; a way of recognising the limits of medicine in the face of nature's infinite power or, which comes to the same thing, the limits of medicine in the face of illness's infinite power.

As soon as he goes into his office, as soon as he closes the door, he begins to tremble. He feels as if, suddenly, his body were breathing differently, making different sounds and movements, as if he bore inside him some helpless, stumbling creature, as if he were giving birth to a disaster. He hurriedly makes his way over to the chair behind the desk and sits down. He's still holding the envelope. Inside are two chest X-rays. Bluish photos, harsh, sharp transparencies. His father's body transformed into a blurred drawing in which, however, death is all too cruelly clear. Andrés feels afraid, even though this isn't a new fear: it's been there for years, stalking him. It must be the same fear which, for no reason and yet so often, leaps out at him from his own shadow. It's the anxiety that weighs on his chest some nights, preventing him from sleeping. We're probably all born with such a fear, which is as vague as it is overwhelming. It wanders about inside us, not knowing where to go, but never leaving us. It prepares itself, trains itself, waiting for the right moment to appear. It's an omen, a voice that doesn't quite know yet what it has to tell us. But it's there, an indecipherable, incomprehensible sound, an insistent drip-drip, an alarm call. He's been hearing it for years, running away from it, trying to frighten it off, but never succeeding. Now, that anxiety has taken on a shape: the face of the radiologist, with its evasive, resigned expression. Andrés has seen it too many times before. He himself must have worn the same expression on more than one occasion. It's the illustration that accompanies a bad diagnosis, the first instalment of an expression of condolence. Is he ready for this? He's not sure.

The phone rings. It's Karina, his secretary. She tells him his father is on the line again, asking if he can speak to him.

"Am I so ill that you don't even want to talk to me?"

This is his father's opening line. Delivered in a jokey tone, of course. Andrés recognises the nervousness that lies behind. It's a classic strategy. Many patients opt to use it, positioning themselves on a thin line where everything is simultaneously half jest and half serious; they try to act normally, when, in fact, they're terrified and haven't stopped thinking, not even for a second, about the possible result of their tests. They've spent hours pursued by the fear of mortal illnesses; they've felt an odd twinge in every movement they make; they've seen suspicious blotches where before they saw only skin. Then they go to the doctor, trying to look strangely natural: they smile, but appear to be on the verge of tears. They ask questions like the one his father has just asked.

"I didn't phone you earlier because I've only just seen the results of your tests," Andrés says.

"And?"

"In principle, everything's fine," he says, touching the sealed edge of the envelope.

3

"In principle? What the hell does that mean, Andrés?"

"Calm down, Dad. I'm telling you that you're fine.'

"You're telling me that, *in principle*, I'm fine: that's rather different."

Andrés is perfectly familiar with this stage too. Generally speaking, patients need to squeeze every word, wringing out its most precise meaning, with every nuance washed away. They want to clear up any doubts, even about punctuation. A patient always suspects that he's not being told the truth or at least not the whole truth, that some information is being withheld. That's why they insist on delving desperately into everything, even language. In this case, though, his father is right. Andrés said "in principle" because he hasn't yet looked at the X-rays. Why doesn't he take them out now, why doesn't he open the envelope and study them? What is stopping him from looking at those results?

The radiologist's face hangs like a balloon in his office. Hospital corridors tend to be full of such balloons. They drift slowly through the air, identical, tenuous bits of plastic on which are painted frowning brows, grave mouths, sober looks: all the outward signs of helpless resignation. It's a ceremony, a clinical protocol. Hospitals are places through which one passes: temples to farewells, monuments to partings.

"I said 'in principle' because I still don't have all the results. The ones I've just been given are fine."

"Which means that …"

"That there's nothing to worry about, Dad," Andrés says, interrupting him, already embarrassed. He can't stand lying for any length of time. "Go out for a walk, have a coffee somewhere with your friends. Everything's fine, really."

"Are you sure?"

"Yes, I'm sure."

There is a brief silence. A tense, unbearable pause. Andrés wants to hang up. He can sense that his father is still uncertain, still in doubt. He can imagine him in his apartment, sitting on the arm of the green sofa beside the phone, gripping the receiver, thinking. Suddenly, Andrés feels as if he were poised above a chasm of nothingness, a precipitous drop. They're suspended for a moment not in silence, but in the void, until:

"You wouldn't lie to me, would you?" His father is speaking from his very bones, in the harsh but intimate voice with which all bones speak. "Andrés," he goes on, "if there was something seriously wrong with me, you wouldn't ever hide it from me, would you?"

Andrés has a hedgehog on his tongue. His throat fills with pineapple rind. Despite himself, his eyes well up with tears. He's afraid his voice might fail him. He makes a huge effort to speak.

"I would never deceive you, Dad," he says at last, with as much conviction as he can manage.

"That's all I wanted to hear. Thank you."

Dear Dr Miranda,

I trust you will remember me. It wasn't easy to get hold of your e-mail address. If you knew what I've been through to find it! But that's another story. What matters is that I'm here now, writing to you. Not that I like the fact. I've never felt comfortable writing. It's not me, it doesn't feel right, I don't know where to put the words or what to say. But in a way, circumstances are forcing me to write. I have no other option.

I need to see you urgently, Doctor. I'm desperate. For three months now, something very strange and mysterious has been going on. When I call your office, I'm told you're not in or can't come to the phone. If I ask to make an appointment, the person at the other end says "No", she can't do that. And she won't explain why either. I'm sure you know nothing about this situation, nothing at all. You would never treat me like that, but if that's the case, who is responsible for all this? And why?

This is the reason for my letter, Doctor. It's the only way I have now of asking you for an appointment. My situation remains the same, with my health deteriorating by the day. Reply directly to this address. Please, trust no-one else. I need to see you as soon as possible.

Thank you for your attention and, as I say, I'm here, waiting for your reply.

Ernesto Durán

Blood is a terrible gossip, it tells everyone everything, as any laboratory technician knows. Hidden inside that dark fluid, stored away in little tubes, lie murky melodramas, characters brought low or sordid stories on the run from the law. When his father fainted, Andrés insisted on him having a whole battery of blood tests. His father protested. He tried to make light of the matter. He preferred the term "dizzy spell" to "fainting fit", and insisted on this almost to the point of absurdity.

"It was just a dizzy spell," he kept repeating, blaming it on the humidity, the summer heat.

It was, according to him, the fault of the climate rather than an indication of some physical ailment. But the truth of the matter is, he had collapsed on the floor like a sack of potatoes in front of the woman who lived in apartment 3-B. They'd been talking about something or other – neither of them could remember what – when suddenly his father collapsed, and the neighbour started screaming hysterically.

"I thought he'd died. He was so pale! Almost blue! I didn't want to touch him because I was afraid he might already be cold! I didn't know what to do! That's why I started screaming!" says the neighbour.

A few seconds later, his father, once he'd recovered consciousness, had tried to calm her down and reassure her that everything was fine, that nothing very grave had happened. Perhaps he had told her, too, that it was just a dizzy spell. Nevertheless, that same afternoon, the neighbour phoned Andrés to let him know what had happened.

"The old busybody!" his father grumbled when Andrés arrived to pick him up and drive him to the hospital.

While the nurse was taking the blood samples, Andrés suddenly noticed that his father had grown smaller. It had never occurred to him before to notice his size, but seeing his father there, arm outstretched, eyes fixed on the ceiling, so as not to have to look at the needle, it seemed to him that his father had become shorter, had lost height. Javier Miranda is a fairly tall man, almost five foot ten. Tall and slim, with a rather athletic build. He always walks very erect, as if his body didn't weigh on him at all. Despite his age and the fact that he's gone grey, he looks cheerful and healthy. His curly hair has won out over any incipient baldness. His skin is slightly tanned, the colour of light clay. His eyes are brown too. He's never smoked, only drinks occasionally, goes for a walk every morning in the park – Parque Los Caobos – avoids fatty foods, has fruit and muesli for breakfast, and every night eats seven raw chickpeas as a way of combatting cholesterol. "What went wrong?" he seemed to be asking himself. He had sidestepped time rather successfully.

Everything had been going relatively well until, one afternoon, that inexplicable fainting fit had stopped him in his tracks. It was that brief wavering of his equilibrium that had brought him to this place and abruptly transformed him into this weak, wounded, small – yes, smaller – person. The words "Sickness is the mother of modesty" came unbidden into Andrés' mind. They appear in Robert Burton's *The Anatomy of Melancholy*, published in 1621. It's required reading in the first term of medical school. The quote bothered him though. It struck him as not so much sad as stupid; behind it lay the desire to make of sickness a virtue. He looked at his father again. Isn't sickness a humiliation rather than a virtue?

Up until now, his father's health had only ever succumbed to the occasional common cold, and a brief urinary infection two years ago, but that was all. He enjoyed enviably good health and, so far, there had been no other worrying signs. Andrés, however, had a bad feeling. The whole situation produced in him a peculiar sense of apprehension. With no evidence on which to base that feeling, he thought for the first time that the worst could happen, that it might already be happening. It irritated him to feel hijacked by a mere hunch, to be taken hostage by something as irrational and unscientific as a bad vibe. His father glanced across at him. Andrés didn't know what to say. It suddenly struck him as pathetic that the fate of a sixty-nine-year-old man could be summed up in just four tubes of dark fluid, O Rh positive. What would his father be feeling at that moment? Resigned? Ready to accept that he was reaching a preordained destiny, that this was a natural conclusion to his life; that now he was entering a stage when people would stick needles in him and when he would inhabit a world dominated by the aseptic smell of laboratories? He again looked hard at his father and was filled by a frightening sense that it was no longer his father meekly putting up with being pricked, touched and bled, it was just a body. Something apart. An older, more vulnerable body in which his father's spirit writhed in protest. Spirit was an odd word. Andrés hadn't used it in ages. He felt that he was using it now for the first time in years.

The two of them. For almost as long as he can remember, it has been just the two of them. His mother died when he was ten. For almost as long as he can remember, Andrés has been the only son of a widower, of a strong man capable of struggling with terrible grief, with great loss. His mother died in an air crash, on a flight from Caracas to Cumaná. The plane was airborne for only a matter of minutes before it nose-dived. It was a national tragedy. The work of the rescue team was hard and, for the most part, fruitless. A special room was set up in the Hospital de La Guaira, where the victims' families could try to identify what little was left: a foot, half a bracelet, the crown of a tooth … His father returned from the hospital that night, looking drawn and ashen. He talked for a while in the kitchen with the other members of the family, then picked up his son and left. Andrés already knew what had happened. Despite his aunts' attempts to protect him, he had managed to elude them and, in secret, had watched the events on television. When his father, his eyes red from crying, went to enormous lengths to soften the news he had to give him and told him that Mama had gone away on a long, long journey, a journey from which she wouldn't come back, Andrés, still confused, fearful and bewildered, simply asked if his mother had been on the plane that had fallen into the sea. His father looked at him uncertainly, then said "Yes" and put his arms around him. Andrés can't be sure now, but he thinks they cried together then.

For a long time, Andrés used to dream about his mother. It was the same dream over and over, with very few variations: the plane was at the bottom of the sea, not like a plane that has crashed, but like a sunken ship; it was quite intact, sleeping among the seaweed and the fish and the shadows, which, like cobwebs, danced across the dull sand. Inside the plane, a large oxygen bubble had formed on the ceiling. It was a very fragile bubble that was slowly shrinking. His mother was trying to swim along with her head inside the bubble so that she could breathe. She appeared to be the sole survivor, there was no-one else, only fish of different colours and sizes that cruised past her with an air of extraordinary, almost bored serenity. It was odd, but in the dream, his mother was wearing a swimsuit and shoes – an orange two-piece swimsuit and a pair of black leather moccasins.

As time passed, his mother grew more desperate. Several times she struck the ceiling of the plane, making a distant, metallic sound, like a tin can being dragged through the sea. She peered out through a window onto nothing, only dark water, a liquid penumbra no eye could penetrate. The sea had no memory, it destroyed everything too quickly for that. Then his mother, beside herself, almost suffocating, beat harder on the ceiling of the plane and cried out: "Andrés! Andrés! I'm alive! Come and get me out of here!"

When he woke, he had usually wet himself and was trembling. Even when he got out of bed, he still felt himself to be in the grip of the dream. It would take him almost a minute to get out of that plane and escape from the bottom of the sea, and stop hearing his mother's cries. His father proved a tireless warrior on his behalf. He patiently helped Andrés to defend himself against those enemies. He was always there, on the edge of the dream, waiting for him.

These memories crowded into his mind as he watched his father in the lab. Did he perhaps have the same presentiment? Andrés would doubtless prefer him not to. When you're nearly seventy, he thought, a bad omen is like a gunshot. At that age, there are no more deadlines, there is only the present.

The nurse removed the needle and handed Javier Miranda a piece of cotton wool soaked in hydrogen peroxide. He pressed down hard on the place where the needle had gone in and glanced at his son as if pleading for a truce, as if asking if they couldn't just get up and leave. Are the monsters of old age as terrible as those that assail us when we're children? What do you dream about when you're sixty-nine? What nightmares recur most often? Perhaps this is what his father dreams about: he's in a laboratory, in the bowels of a hospital, surrounded by chemicals, sharp implements, gauze, and strangers all repellently dressed in white; yes, he's in the bowels of a hospital, looking for a tiny bubble of air, so that he can breathe, so that he can shout: "Andrés! Andrés! Get me out of here! Save me!"

While Andrés was driving his father home, he tried to avoid talking about the subject. It wasn't easy. His father kept muttering bitterly to himself. He claimed that the tests were a complete waste of time, that the only thing they would show was that his cholesterol levels were slightly raised, if that. Certainly nothing more, he insisted. Andrés dropped him off at the door to his apartment building. As he was driving away, he could still see his father in the rear-view mirror. There had been a time when he had considered having his father move in with them, but had feared that family life might become a nightmare for everyone. Mariana got on reasonably well with his father, and his children

11

had a lot of fun with him, but those were only sporadic encounters, occasional trips to the cinema or to a park, to a restaurant or to a baseball game. Day-to-day life is a different matter, a far more demanding exercise. And yet, at that moment, while he could still see him, a diminutive figure in the rear-view mirror, he again considered the possibility. Sooner or later, if you were an only child, you had to pay for your exclusivity. His father had no-one else. If, instead of standing in the corridor, talking to the neighbour, he had been alone in his apartment, it could have been really serious. For a second, Andrés sees the scene with hideous clarity: his father goes into the kitchen to turn off the gas under the coffee-pot, he bends over, loses consciousness and collapses. In the same movement, in the inertia of the fall, his head drops forward, propelled by the weight of his body. It strikes the edge of the stove, then the handle on the oven and, finally, the tiled floor. The green veins in his forehead are swollen and tense. His nose is broken. His right eye looks slightly sunken and there is blood on his right cheekbone. There's more blood above his right eyebrow. He could have broken a rib: perhaps, when he comes to, he won't be able to move or call anyone. The water is boiling. Soon there will be the smell of burnt coffee.

That night, Andrés would have liked to make love with Mariana. Not for any special reason and without even feeling any particular desire for her, but he needed to have sex. It was a need, a furious longing to be on top of her, penetrating her, without thinking about anything, without saying anything, just following the urgent pistoning of hips, the rise and fall. But he didn't know how to approach her. He wasn't in the mood to seduce her and felt ashamed to say what he really wanted. Women don't understand that for men sex is sometimes a sport, one they can practise at any time, at any moment and with anyone. Masculinity is too basic, too simple. The love ethic tends to be feminine.

"Don't you think you're blowing things up out of all proportion?" Mariana asked before they went to sleep. "You don't even know the results of the tests yet. Why are you getting so upset?"

Andrés reminds her that his father has become rather forgetful lately. Every detail now begins to take on a new importance for him, a new value.

"Even you commented on it recently," he says. "We were here, having a meal."

"Yes, true. But that's normal, isn't it? Even I forget things sometimes, so why shouldn't your father? Don't exaggerate. Why insist on thinking the worst?".

He doesn't know why, he certainly didn't know then. But he had that incomprehensible, unpleasant feeling, as if some fatal, imminent event were circling him, the intuition that what had happened to his father that day was the first sign of something much more serious and definitive: Burkitt's lymphoma, for example, or a cutaneous mucinous carcinoma, or an asymptomatic neoplasy of plasma cells. Andrés knows perfectly well that nature translates those words in the most pitiless way. What terrifies him most is imagining his father suffering. His father hunched and screaming, racked with pain and weeping. Pain is the most terrible of the body's languages. A grammar of screams. A prolonged howl.

He left Mariana reading in bed and went out onto the balcony. It annoyed him that he should start believing in presentiments. A doctor with a PhD in immunology and almost twenty years' professional experience has no right to have presentiments. Susan Sontag said that there are two kingdoms:

sickness and health. Human beings often have to move between the two. Andrés has often thought that in the middle, on the frontier of those two geographies, stand the doctors, checking passports, asking questions, weighing things up. They may have their suspicions, but they need proof. It's a job that requires evidence. A doctor sees erythema, hematoma, cells, enzymes, proteic variables; a doctor reads symptoms and takes no notice of vibes, hunches, fleeting images.

The sound of the telephone ringing was like an aluminium finger scraping the air. He answered at once. It was the laboratory. The test results he had asked for as a matter of urgency were ready. While he listened to the figures, noting them down on a piece of paper, he continued to feel the same anxiety. It was as if a voracious, insatiable animal had taken up residence inside him and was still there, panting, even when he could see that all the results were normal. Just as his father had said, the only thing wrong was a slightly raised cholesterol level. Everything else was fine, within the usual range. He glanced at his watch and decided that it wasn't too late to call his father. Not that he was in celebratory mood. The wretched presentiment refused to go away, it wasn't satisfied. There is always some piece of gossip over which the blood has no control. He picked up the phone and rang the hospital again. He booked an appointment first thing the next morning to take some chest X-rays and do a C.T. scan. He didn't want to leave any room for doubt.

Why does he insist on thinking the worst?

Because sometimes the worst happens.

It wasn't easy to persuade his father to go back to the hospital. Andrés almost had to drag him there. He immediately got upset and went on the defensive. Andrés showed him the blood-test results and assured him that everything was fine, but his father reacted as anyone else would have:

"If everything's fine, why are you making me go for more tests?"

There was no alternative. Andrés had to sit down and tell him straight: yes, the blood tests were fine, but he wanted to be absolutely sure, that's why he thought his father should have a couple of X-rays and an M.R.I. scan. It was part of a general examination, a routine exercise, simply to confirm that everything was alright.

"Trust me," he said. "Believe me."

His father sighed deeply and only then agreed to be taken to the hospital's radiology unit.

His father comes out into the corridor and eyes him gloomily. His naked body is covered only by one of those skimpy gowns that tie at the back. Andrés almost runs over to him.

"There, that wasn't so bad, was it?"

His father doesn't answer. He doesn't even look at him now. He could at least grunt a response.

"Now there's just the M.R.I. and the C.T. scan," murmurs Andrés, about to propel his father down the corridor.

His father complies, still without looking at him.

"When someone faints," Andrés explains again, "there has to be a motive, a reason, a cause. That's what medicine is for. If the blood tests don't give me an answer, then I have to try something else. That's all. That's all it is. A matter of searching for answers."

"He who seeks, finds," his father mutters reproachfully and continues on down the corridor, still refusing to look at him.

*

Dear Dr Miranda,

Did my e-mail not reach you? I'm a bit of a novice on the Internet, perhaps I pressed the wrong button. I've been thinking about this while I've been waiting. I keep checking my in-box to see if there's a message from you, but there never is.

Meanwhile, I haven't even attempted to phone you. The last time, your secretary told me that those were your instructions, that you yourself had told her not to put me through, that you had even asked hospital security not to let me in if I should show my face there. I don't believe it, I said. I can't believe it. And she hung up. I haven't phoned since. But I'm still worried, Doctor, I don't understand what's going on. There's no logical explanation for all this. That's why I persist, that's why it's so important that I write you another letter, that's why it's so important that you should answer.

It also occurred to me that perhaps you don't remember me. Is that the reason? It seems rather odd, but then again it might explain why you haven't yet responded. Or perhaps you're confusing me with someone else. That's another possibility. I've spent the last few days going over and over all this in my mind. You probably don't remember most of the people who pass through your office. How many patients do you see a day? Seven, eight, ten, twelve? Possibly more. Multiplied by the five days of the week, of course. That's a lot of people. You probably think no-one could remember that many people. But I'm sure no-one forgets you. For us, you're the doctor. Our doctor. My doctor. For you, we're just patients in general, anonymous beings, your patients, people who wait to be seen. The word says it all – patients – people who are patient. For us, on the other hand, you have a first and a last name. You're Dr Andrés Miranda. You're unique.

I'm worried now that you'll take what I've just written the wrong way. I hope not. I'm only saying all this because it has to do with my relationship with you. If I may, I'm going to remind you of our first meeting. I found out about you while I was visiting another doctor, in one of those medical journals you get in waiting rooms. I read an article you'd written about the relationship between doctors and patients. You said, and I'm sure you'll remember this, that it was part of the treatment, that the relationship between doctor and patient could contribute to the healing process. You said that we shouldn't speak of illness but of ill people. That illness, in general terms, did not exist. That only individual people, ill people, existed, and that the relationship between doctor and patient should be a personal as well as a medical one.

That idea made such an impact on me that I immediately looked you up so that I could come and see you, so that you could be my doctor. I told you all this during our first appointment. And you listened to me very attentively. At least that's how it felt. I felt that you were really listening to me. We talked about my job at the telephone company. We talked about my life, my family, my parents, my brothers and sisters. I told you about my divorce, about how badly I got on with my ex-wife, and still do. Then we moved on to the physical symptoms. You were very attentive about those too. I felt you were listening to me with genuine and profound interest, with respect. I tried to explain in detail what was going on.

17

Since I don't know whether you remember or not, I feel I should repeat it all here. If you don't mind, it's your turn to be patient.

For some time, I've been experiencing sudden drops in blood pressure, an internal imbalance which means that, on a daily basis, I frequently feel as if I were on the verge of fainting. The symptoms are quite clear: cold sweats, pallor, a feeling of inner weakness, a decrease in body temperature, and, of course, the slight dizziness anyone experiences before a fainting fit. I told you all this. And you noted everything down. You asked a few questions. Then you checked me over, took my blood pressure, "120 over 80," you said, adding: "Very good." Then I mentioned the article I'd read and told you that was the reason I'd come to see you. You just smiled. I swear to you I felt sure I'd finally found a doctor I could trust.

At our next appointment, and you're bound to remember this, I arrived with the results of the tests you'd advised me to have done. A complete blood count and a lipid profile. You were just as friendly as you were the first time. We even joked a little, talking about my ex-wife, about women and ex-wives in general. I felt we were making some progress in our relationship. You told me that you were married and had two children. I told you that, fortunately, I hadn't had any children during my failed marriage. Anyway, then we got down to medical matters. You said that the test results were excellent and that I was fine. That was impossible, I told you. I was still getting the dizzy spells. Perhaps you didn't like me being so insistent. But I had to do it. I was the one who was going to faint, not you. In fact, I said just that.

Then you assured me that I was in perfect health. That I wasn't going to faint. That it was a physical impossibility. On that occasion, you asked me to believe you, to trust you. And I did, Dr Miranda. Now I'm the one asking the same thing of you: believe me, have faith in me, trust me . . . please, answer me!

Hoping to hear from you soon.

Sincerely,

Ernesto Durán

When Miguel arrives, Andrés is already sitting at a table slightly apart from the other tables, drinking his second whisky and ice. Miguel looks harassed and preoccupied.

"Sorry I'm late," he says as he sits down.

Andrés merely makes a vague movement with his head, neither a nod nor a shake, as if hoping, nonetheless, to communicate something by that gesture. His face almost breathes unease and distress.

"On the phone you said it was something serious," says Miguel, "but now that I see your face, I feel quite frightened. Whatever's happened?"

Andrés points to the two envelopes on the table.

"Have a look at those," he says, almost in a murmur.

Miguel picks up one envelope, takes out the X-rays and holds them up to the light. First, those showing the lungs, then the images from the brain scans.

"There's no mistaking the signs. There's no other way to read them," says Andrés. "Or is there?"

Miguel turns towards him, tense, not sure what to answer. The waiter approaches and before he can say anything, Andrés cuts in with:

"He'll have a vodka with ice and lemon. A double," he tells him emphatically, deliberately, his eyes fixed on Miguel.

"I have to perform a fistula operation this afternoon," Miguel says in answer to a question no-one has asked, although he doesn't sound very convinced.

"Just tell me what you think. There's no hope, is there?"

Miguel doesn't so much sigh as snort, before turning back to the X-rays. He again holds them up to the light, looking at them almost obliquely. The contrast between the blue and the opaque white reveals spots, dark irruptions, shadows that should not be there.

"It's a spinocellular carcinoma, isn't it?" Miguel asks, still scrutinising the results of the scans.

"Stage IV," says Andrés. Then he points to one of the C.T. images. "With cerebral metastasis," he adds, his voice breaking.

"Whose X-rays are they?" Miguel asks rather fearfully, looking straight at him now.

"My dad's," says Andrés.

They sit staring at each other for a moment, not saying a word, wrapped in that rare complicity that comes with friendship.

"Shit!" is all Miguel can manage to say after that pause.

Andrés quickly talks him through the sequence of events: first, the fainting fit, then his own presentiment, the results of the blood tests, that presentiment again, the chest X-rays and the C.T. scans. Miguel tries to get more details, to find other possible explanations.

"If he weren't my father," Andrés says, "you and I would have looked at the plates and concluded that there was no hope, that it's the mother of all tumours, that the patient is basically screwed," he adds, his voice choked with emotion. "There's no need for a biopsy, there's no point in opening him up."

"Maybe, but . . ." Miguel would like to say something, but there's nothing to say. He can't fool Andrés.

"Why do we find it so hard to accept that life is a matter of chance?" Andrés asks suddenly, a lump in his throat.

They both fall silent. Another whisky, another vodka. Miguel makes a phone call to cancel that afternoon's operation. Andrés puts the X-rays and C.T. images back in their envelopes.

"And your dad, of course, knows nothing."

"No."

"You're not going to be so stupid as to tell him, are you?"

"That's what I always do, isn't it? It's what I've always said, the position I've always defended: the transparent relationship between doctor and patient."

Another silence. Then Miguel tells him that he's never agreed with that approach. Andrés nods, as if he hadn't heard him, as if it were merely a mechanical, involuntary movement made while his mind is elsewhere. Perhaps he's listening to his memory, watching all the sick people he's treated and their families parade past; seeing all those who were going to die and for whom there was no hope. Perhaps he's remembering how he put into practice his theory of transparency. Some people even found him hard and inhuman. Others thanked him. Andrés always preferred to share the clinical truth with the objects of that truth, with those weary bodies, transformed into medical material, the recipients of needles and chemicals. It had often fallen to him to say: "I'm sorry, there's no hope. There's not even any point trying somewhere else, going to Los Angeles or Houston. You have, at most, two months to live."

He has always insisted that it's best to be completely open with a patient. Even at the risk of inoculating him or her with a fear as terrible as the sickness itself. The likelihood is that the patient already suspects it, senses it, is secretly listening to the warnings coming from his or her own body, to the final note sounded by the sickness.

"We all have the right to know that our life has an end-date, a deadline; we all have a right to know when and how we will die, that's what I've always said."

"But now it's your father who's on the other end of the stethoscope. It's absurd, Andrés, think about it. You and I know how fast a cancer like this spreads."

"And he's never even smoked, damn it!" mutters Andrés. "Not a single bloody cigarette in all his life!" he exclaims, pressing his lips together, as if he had bitten on an ice cube.

"That's what I mean. Don't you think he's going to say precisely the same thing and ask the same question? What point is there in him knowing the truth?"

"I can't deceive him now. It wouldn't be right."

"I'm sorry, but that's total bullshit."

"No, it's not. It's part of our history, part of what we've been through together, as father and son."

"The big question is: can you do it?" While he speaks, Miguel fidgets on his chair, leans forward, gives a certain confidential tone to his words. "I mean, it's easier to say such things to a patient, to someone who isn't a member of your family. It's upsetting, but it's not the same; it's different having your father there before you, and having to say to him: 'Dad, you've only got a few more weeks to live.' That's what I mean. Can you do that?"

"No, I can't."

Miguel nods, picks up his glass and takes another thoughtful sip before glancing first at his watch and then back at Andrés.

22

"Let me tell you about a case we had in the department recently," he says at last.

Miguel is a nephrologist and, as well as having a private practice, he has worked for years as the director of a dialysis unit in a state-run hospital.

"There's this one patient, he's sixty-eight, a grumpy old thing called Efraín. He's a diabetic, at least that's his main ailment. He's in the final stages, his kidneys are pretty much buggered, and he's nearly blind. He has a terrible time on the dialysis machine. He screams and cries. He drives the technicians and the nurses mad. He's become very bitter and fed up with life. Worse still: living for him equals suffering. He has to come into the unit three times a week and follow a ghastly diet, he finds walking very difficult and his life expectancy is reducing by the day, so you can imagine what his life is like. One afternoon, one of the nurses asked if she could speak to me alone. I was a bit puzzled by this at first, but we went into the office and sat down. Then she told me that Efraín wanted to die. I was really surprised. I thought perhaps she might be joking. Of course he must want to die, but the tone in which she said it implied something else. She said again that he wanted to die, that he was fed up with the whole business and tired of living like that. In principle, the procedure was simple: he just had to stop coming for dialysis. That's all he needed to do. If, for one reason or another, he stayed at home, that would be that. His body wouldn't be able to stand it, some organ would simply stop working and he would die. You could almost call it a natural death."

Andrés nods silently. He signs to the waiter and asks for another whisky.

"That's what the guy wants," Miguel goes on. "He just wants the nightmare to end. So do his family. They've had enough, they're as ill as he is. His illness has infected them, it's killing *them* as well. They've spent years in the same hideous situation. You know what it's like. The man can't do anything for himself now, he's half-blind, he stinks of bicarbonate from the machine, he has to take special medicines; they have to ferry him back and forth, keep an eye on his blood pressure, feed him, wash him . . . Viewed coldly and objectively, for his family it would be a great relief, in every sense, if he were to die. And there's another point too: if you consider the situation from an institutional point of view, from the point of view of providing a public service, it would suit society as well if old Efraín were to die. You and I have discussed this kind of thing before. He's nearly seventy and, given his age and state of health, he has no chance of being selected for a kidney transplant. But he's taking up a place, a turn, on a dialysis machine. At the time, there was a seventeen-year-old girl on the list, waiting for a chance to start treatment at the unit. Wouldn't it be fairer for that girl to be there, rather than Efraín? I know that someone else, hearing this same story, might think it was tantamount to sanctioning homicide or murder or assisted suicide. But at the time, we all thought that Efraín's death could be a blow for justice as far as the girl and her family were concerned and for Efraín as well. As you yourself said: he already knew what his end-date, his deadline, was. All he wanted was to exercise his right to hasten that moment and not to continue this painful, long-drawn-out death. I talked to a priest about all this once. He, of course, gave me a sermon. I waited, and when he'd finished, I asked him: is masochism a sin? He was surprised, he hesitated, and then he said, yes, it was. Well, Efraín didn't want to go on sinning. Living, for him, was a masochistic act. He simply wanted his death to be a gentle one, he wanted his death to put an end to the torment of his life."

"What are you getting at with all this? What did you do?"

"Do you know what happened? We decided to take the risk. All of us in the unit. If anyone had found out, we would have been in big trouble. The media would have had a field day, but that didn't frighten us; we decided to take the risk anyway. I took it on myself to speak to Efraín's family, to his wife and his eldest daughter. It was rather awkward, as you can imagine, one of those conversations in which no-one says exactly what they mean; we spoke as if in code. There was a silent, secret pact. Efraín agreed to it too. He would go home, stop coming to dialysis, and that would be that. But it came to nothing. It all fell flat. And do you know why? Because we needed a signature, we needed one member of Efraín's family to sign a piece of paper, saying that Efraín Salgado had stopped coming to the dialysis unit of his own free will. It was just a way of protecting ourselves, so that no-one else in his family could come to us later and accuse the unit of refusing to help a patient."

"And what happened?"

"No-one would sign! Not one of his relatives would dare! They felt that by signing that piece of paper, they were confessing to a crime. And it was that one apparently foolish, trivial thing that brought the whole plan crashing down. What I considered to be a mere bureaucratic detail, a mere formality once we had sorted out the really important matter, became for them a kind of definitive symbol. The person who signed that paper would somehow be responsible for his death, would have Efraín's corpse on his or her conscience. As if scribbling your name on a sheet of paper would immediately convert that act into a crime. At least, I think that's what they felt. They needed to be able to turn a blind eye, they needed everything to happen as if by chance, as if it really were unintentional. They needed to feel that the old man was dying of his own accord, without any of them knowing anything about it.'

Miguel orders some curried prawns. Andrés isn't hungry, he sits there mute and absent. His mobile phone rings. He checks to see who's calling and decides not to answer. The phone continues to ring on the table. It's a pointless, futile sound. Andrés doesn't offer an explanation, he just sits and says nothing. Miguel looks at him and suddenly feels rather embarrassed.

"I don't really know why that story came into my mind," he says, somewhat regretfully. "I don't know why I told it to you. What connection does it have with your father and with what we've been talking about?'

"I'm not sure," says Andrés. "But perhaps there is a connection."

Miguel shakes his head.

"No, I just suddenly remembered it and felt like telling you, although now I really don't know why. I'm sorry."

Deep down, Miguel would like to take back that anecdote, to feel around on the floor for the crumbs of that story and return it intact to his memory. What made him think of it? Why had he got so carried away and told Andrés? It really wasn't what his friend needed just then. It wasn't what he was hoping for from him. He had asked to meet in order to tell him that his father has cancer, that his father's going to die, and instead of being supportive and consoling, there he was telling him that macabre tale about a man who wants to die and about a wife and children who want their husband and father to die as well. Why? What for?

"Don't worry, it's alright." Andrés shakes his head again. His eyes are sad, but he's smiling slightly.

"No, it's not alright. There you are, in a state of complete shock and what do I do? I start telling you some entirely irrelevant story."

The waiter comes over with the bill, and the usual battle of the credit cards ensues, the battle to decide who pays. Miguel insists on making the bill his penance, and he wins. When the waiter leaves, Andrés says to Miguel.

"I know what made you think of that story."

Miguel listens, but continues to shake his head.

"Basically," Andrés goes on, "your memory came up with a story about how dying isn't as easy as it seems. That sometimes knowing what's happening or about to happen doesn't help. Nothing more. The word 'death' casts a very unpredictable spell. 'Keep the truth from your dad. Don't tell your dad the truth', that's what you were saying."

While Miguel makes a visit to the toilets, Andrés thinks that perhaps this is one of the most tragic consequences of illness: it destroys all other appearances, it won't allow death to dissemble, it ruins any chance of death taking place as if nothing at all or else something entirely different were happening.

By six, Andrés is on his way back home, caught up in a terrible tailback on the motorway heading to the south of the city. All five lanes are completely blocked. It's the typical urban image that appears to fascinate so many people: hordes of cars, one after the other, all breathing slowly beneath the indifferent, mustard-coloured sun. For the first time in that whole painful situation, Andrés doesn't feel gripped by ill temper or by the need to get home as soon as possible and to have a sense that the day is finally over. Perhaps it's the effect of the whisky. On the passenger seat lie his father's X-rays. Andrés is briefly aware of them in his peripheral vision. He closes his eyes. Only for a second. His eyelids feel stiff and painful. He knows what's going to happen and that it's inevitable. In a stupid, futile gesture, he turns on the radio, trying to stop the unstoppable. He flips from station to station, but they're of no use, those intersecting voices and songs. He can already feel the tears pricking at the edges of his pupils. It's unpleasant. It stings. He's crying, but he'd also like to scream, to thump the steering wheel. His saliva has grown thick. He can't hold back now, he can't stop crying. He doesn't know how.

Dear Dr Miranda,

I don't know how much longer I'll have to wait for an answer. I thought that, after my second letter, you would reply within a day or two. Not so. I've been making some enquiries and I've been told that e-mails do sometimes go astray, that it often happens. This means that perhaps you did reply to me, but your reply got lost and ended up in someone else's in-box, for example. It also occurred to me that perhaps it would be best if I printed out these letters and went in person to the hospital to give them to you. Although, before I do that, I would much prefer it if we could get this system to work and you could at least tell me whether or not you've received my messages. That's all I need: for you to send a letter with a "Yes" or a "No", nothing more, just that. Then at least I'd know we were in touch.

While I've been waiting for your response, I've been considering our relationship and trying to recall if there was anything I did that might have offended you, that could possibly have produced a reaction like this. Is it possible that you receive and read my letters, but don't wish to answer me, that you want nothing more to do with me? Is what your secretary says right? I've gone over and over it in my mind and that just doesn't seem possible. It doesn't make sense. You couldn't do that to a sick man. At least, that's how I feel, how I still feel.

As I mentioned in my previous letter, all I ask of you is a little of the same trust I placed in you. You told me I was in perfect health, that there was no way I would faint, and I trusted you. And I did actually feel better for a day or two. On the third day, though, the dizzy spells came back. I remember it perfectly. I was leaving work and was walking down Avenida Solano. It was midday and very hot and sunny. I was feeling perfectly fine, when, suddenly, at a corner of the street, I was gripped again by the same symptoms. I was terrified. I thought I would collapse right there and then. My hands were cold, my head was sweating and I found it hard to swallow. I had the sense that everything around me was about to start moving, that I was losing my balance. That was the first time I phoned you. I didn't know what else to do. Surely you remember. I told you it was an emergency, I explained what was happening. You were really surprised. I'm sure you remember that. You told me to stay calm and to describe what I was feeling. I was in such a state. I told you I was going to faint. Then all I could do was hail a passing taxi, bundle myself inside and ask to be taken at once to A&E. I know you were a bit put out on that occasion. You showed me all the test results. Everything was normal. I was fine. I didn't know what to say. But I felt safe in the hospital, knowing you were near and that if anything happened to me, you would be there for me.

True, it was a particularly difficult time for me, I was

in a really bad way, anxious and out of control. And it wasn't a good idea to start phoning you from different places in the city, at different times, so that you could calm me down and reassure me that I wasn't going to faint. But that really *is* what I felt, that if I didn't talk to you, I would pass out wherever I happened to be. I felt that I depended on you, that you were my guarantee that I wouldn't collapse on the floor that very instant.

I have no words to describe it, and, believe me, that inability drives me to despair. I don't know how to get across to you the terrible, physical certainty that I was about to pass out, to faint. There was a ravine inside my body. That sounds odd, I know, but that's how it was. I was deathly pale, and even though I couldn't see my face, I knew how pale I was. I could feel the blood pounding in my temples. The tips of my fingers were ice-cold. It wasn't all in my imagination. I never *liked* having to bother you, interrupt you, hound you. The truth is I really regret having done so. I simply wanted to communicate to you what it was I was experiencing with such intensity. That's why I insisted on further investigations, on a more in-depth medical evaluation. I can't deny that, at the time, your behaviour remained exemplary, very wise and patient. You were invariably friendly and pleasant, but you never swerved in your diagnosis. You listened to me, but you took no notice of me, and that's why sometimes I really despaired. And then came the afternoon when you said you wanted to talk to me frankly. And I thought to myself: At last! But you surprised me. Instead of listening to me, instead of dealing with my pressing problems, you told me that you didn't want me to continue wasting my time and my money, do you remember? I'm sure you must remember that. You told me that I didn't need you, that I didn't need a medical doctor, but a psychiatrist.

That same afternoon, you suggested I go into therapy. You even recommended a lady doctor, a friend of yours, and gave me the number of her practice. And again I took your advice. You see what confidence I had in you! I did as you suggested and went to the therapist you recommended. I'm not sure why, but I think that was when our problems began. From that moment on, everything between us changed, and I've never again been able to speak to you.

I've even wondered if perhaps the psychiatrist told you what we talked about at our first meeting. Perhaps that was it. As soon as I left her office, she picked up the phone and dialled your number. At least that's what I imagine happened now. Although that still doesn't make sense, I mean, what could she have told you that was so very dreadful? I don't remember having said anything unusual that day. I arrived punctually, but I have to say, I took an instant dislike to the woman, she seemed so cold, unfriendly, distant. She didn't even try to break the ice, as they say. She didn't speak at all. She just sat there in silence, and I realised that it was up to me to talk. I told her a little about what had happened, why I was there. I talked about you and my fainting fits. But she still said nothing. Occasionally, she scribbled something in her notebook. I felt uncomfortable, well, I didn't have much more to tell. I asked her: What else do you want to know? What more do I need to say? And she said that this was my time and I could say what I liked. That made me feel even more uncomfortable. The fact is I didn't like that therapy business at all. What was I doing there? Why was I having to talk to that stranger? What was I supposed to do? Talk about my life, my intimate thoughts, to a woman I'd only just met? And I was paying for it too! During the rest of the session, I just kept telling her about my fainting fits, but nothing more.

But something must have happened, Doctor, and it's either that psychiatrist or your secretary who's to blame, because I haven't managed to speak to you since or get another appointment. Do you see? It makes me think that perhaps you've been kidnapped, that someone is holding you against your will so that we can't meet. That's what I feel.

I didn't finish this letter last night. I was tired, and it was late. I don't think I knew quite how to continue. It's odd. I had the feeling that I should stop, but I couldn't find a way to end it, if you see what I mean. I got up early this morning, went for a walk, ate a little fruit and sat down to finish this letter before going to work. I have to confess, Doctor, that I'm starting to feel really frustrated. What if you don't answer this letter either? If there's no answer, what should I do? I'm still getting the dizzy spells. In fact, they're getting worse and worse. Now my saliva's gone funny too. I have a bitter taste in my mouth all the time. I've also started to feel a kind of pressure around my eyes, on my eyelids. These are new symptoms, Doctor. I'm afraid that when we do at last meet and talk, when we do see each other again, it will be too late.
Ernesto Durán

*

Mariana is white, but not too white, not so white as to be just that, a white woman. He thinks this while he watches her naked in the shower. Andrés has closed the door and sat down on the lid of the toilet. She hasn't spotted him there yet. Reality is always different when you're taking a shower. She is simply there, letting the water do what it will with her, as if nothing else existed, as if the steam were not something impermanent, as if the world was not just outside that room, as close to hand as her towel. Neither the years nor the children have made her less desirable. Not, at least, to him. Ever since the research carried out by Dr Winnifred Cutler in 1986, science has been doing its best to dissect desire, even concluding that what people call love, physical love, has a shelf-life, and can't last more than seven years. Andrés' own experience contradicts such statements. He looks at Mariana and feels a tremor inside him, a tension. Desire consumes the body, but doesn't wear it down. It doesn't grow wrinkled; it changes, it's transformed, but doesn't age. He looks at Mariana now and he desires her. Tonight, even when he's depressed and tired, even after fourteen years together, desire remains undefeated. He likes her. He likes her small, narrow shoulders. He likes her size, her skin, her bottom, her feet, her cunt. He has been inside that body so many times and yet it still excites him to see her naked.

"How long have *you* been there?" she asks when she finally notices him.

Andrés doesn't answer. He pulls her towards him, gently takes her towel from her and starts to dry her.

"What's up? What happened with your dad?"

He continues absentmindedly running the towel over Mariana's body. Confronted by such silence, she finally turns to

33

look him in the eye.

"What happened?" she asks again.

"I don't want to talk now," mutters Andrés, before leaning towards her, in search of a kiss, as if wanting to murder words, to erase them with his lips, to wall them in.

They made love in the bathroom. Furiously. Like young things. She squatted over him, her back to him. Andrés bit her neck, her shoulders. They made love like two cats. They both enjoyed powerful orgasms and were left panting and silent, as if each body were taking a while to return to its place. Then they went into the bedroom, where they lay down naked on the bed and talked. Andrés had felt nothing special when he first met her. Nor had Mariana. It wasn't love at first sight, or even second or third. But a taste, an inner liking hovered and grew around them, until one night, at a friend's house, much as had happened just now, except that then they had drunk too much wine, they wearied of watching a Russian film on video and went off into another room. There they started talking, recognised their mutual attraction and, without quite knowing how, started to take off their clothes between kisses and caresses. They clutched and clung to each other. They had sex the way two strangers, two bodies, usually have sex for the first time, bodies that have not yet constructed their own intimacy. Then they spent all night talking, sitting naked on the granite floor. That is perhaps what they most remember about that first time – the cold of the granite on their buttocks.

"Dad has cancer," Andrés says.

Those words, hard and all of a piece, fall onto the bed. They lie down between them. Mariana is surprised, taken aback. She doesn't know how to react.

"It's lung cancer."

"But . . ."

"There's nothing to be done," adds Andrés, making a great effort. Each word weighs on him, hurts him, tastes of glass.

"That's not possible. We have to do something," she says, shaken, moving her naked body closer to his.

"We can do all the usual things – chemo, radiotherapy. But it's stage IV. It's spread. He has metastasis to the brain."

"Oh God!" is all Mariana manages to say, like an exhalation, before covering her face with her hands and breaking into sobs.

Andrés puts his arms around her. He, too, would have preferred to use a different term, less definitive, less final. Suddenly, that stumbling of one "t" against another, that precipice of "s"s in the word "metastasis", leaves them clinging to each other, unable to speak, simply crying.

Tears are very unliterary: they have no form.

"Are you going to tell him?"

"I don't know."

Mariana pulls on her dressing gown and goes into the kitchen to get a glass of water. Andrés still isn't hungry. He rolls over so that he's lying on his back, still naked, gazing up at the ceiling. This was almost a sport for him when he was an adolescent and used to spend hours staring at the ceiling. He can even remember the different lamps he had in the different bedrooms of the many apartments he lived in with his father. His father liked moving. That, over time, is the only explanation he has found. Every two years, Javier Miranda would be seized by a strange restlessness, by an uncontrollable enthusiasm for new property. He would search the classified ads for a new place to live, another apartment to rent. He did this with such intense interest that Andrés came to feel that each move was a journey to another country, a marvellous excursion. Instead of taking holidays, they moved apartments.

After the accident, his father never again boarded a plane. Never. Andrés remembers this now. He also remembers that he himself had to overcome the same fear. He was always looking for an excuse not to travel, until his wedding and the honeymoon, which Mariana was reluctant to spend on the Venezuelan plains. Thanks to an uncle who owned a travel agency, she had been offered a bargain break in the Dominican Republic. Before Andrés even had a chance to confess his fears, she had the air tickets in her hand. On the outward journey, he took 6 milligrams of bromazepam, and on the homeward flight, he drank a whole bottle of rum. He spent the four days in between shaking. Each time he remembered that he would have to get on a plane again, he was gripped by terrible anxiety. The Dominican Republic was an exception, and had it not been for therapy, it would have remained the one exception of his life. He would never have gone on any holidays abroad, he would never have attended any medical conferences held outside Venezuela. He would only have known places one could reach by car. That was his father. That was Javier Miranda now. Almost seventy years old and with lung cancer.

Andrés lies there naked and staring up at the ceiling: when he was an adolescent, he associated that position with having a good wank, with the ritual of masturbation. Age has its advantages. Masturbation is a generous, irreplaceable act that develops self-esteem and promotes good health; nevertheless, it can't compare with the satisfaction of having sex with a partner. The best orgasms are always to be had with someone else. It was only when he met Mariana, and they both became experts in the art, one with the other, that Andrés began to experience really profound orgasms, real festivals of tremors and tremblings, of indescribable chemical discharges. Sometimes, when he ejaculated, the feeling was so strong that he felt that blood not semen was being expelled from his penis. Physical ecstasy is inevitably and marvellously bound up with dirt and the idea of dirtiness. Baudelaire believed this was a condition of love. "We are," he wrote, "reduced to making love with the excremental organs."

Mariana is back. She's carrying a glass of water and looking thoughtful. All this time, she has been pondering the same question, which she can't shake off: "Are you going to tell him?"

In the early hours, the same question haunts Andrés. It buzzes like a mosquito in his ear, alights on his left cheek, almost dances on one eyelid. He's done everything he can to shoo it away, but it's very insistent. He goes to his shelves and searches out a book by the Mexican doctor Arnoldo Kraus, *A Reading of Life*, in which he recalls coming across an analysis of the conflict between those who think that "telling the patient everything can be counterproductive" and those who think "it's unethical to withhold information". He skims the pages while Mariana, still naked, sleeps beside him. He knows he's not going to find any magic recipe or instruction or order. Or even advice. Dying should always be a simple act: there's nothing simpler than a massive heart attack. The difficulty lies in what is not yet over, in sickness. It's the experience of loss brought to a climax, to a threshold from which there's no return. Is it really necessary for his father to know the truth? What advantage would that bring him? What can he do with that information? What use is it for him to know that his body is betraying him, that very soon he will die?

Andrés can analyse the effect of this news on himself. Since he saw the scan of his father's brain until now, until this rumpled dawn moment, how has he felt? Tense, nervous. He's

37

filled with a sense of haste, of hurry and anxiety. It's an inner despair, almost liquid, that never ceases to boil, to flow, to stain everything. His memory is permanently startled. Memories, images, anecdotes come and go all the time. It's as if the past had been let out of a box. He is now pure, stampeding fear. Would it be the same for his father? Would all the memories of his nearly seventy years rush into his mind? Would that be the best way to say goodbye to life?

Andrés reads an extract from Kraus' book: "In fact, it isn't at all easy to tell which patients will be capable of being told everything and which will not. It's a complicated business determining who will benefit from knowing how long it will be before they go blind, before they cease being able to walk or require catheters to ensure that their sphincters continue to function. And yet it's clear that there are some people capable of handling bad news and others who simply can't." Which group does Javier Miranda, his father, belong to? Was it possible to place him, with exactitude, among those who know how to handle "bad news"? A piece of fateful, not to say final news? Perhaps Miguel was right: it's not possible to guess how one human being will react when he discovers how close he is to death. That strong, determined man called Javier Miranda might, despite all predictions to the contrary, collapse and break down when faced with that scan of his brain and the glowing spots devouring it.

Dear Dr Miranda,
I have a confession to make: I'm following you.

Up until then, up until she read those words, Karina has thought of Ernesto Durán as a mere curiosity. She has read his previous e-mails with a smile on her face. Dr Miranda's secretary is in charge of anything that arrives in his electronic in-box. It's intended exclusively for professional correspondence. He tends to get a lot of promotional material from medical laboratories and pharmaceutical companies, as well as invitations to work-related activities – meetings, official functions, book launches, conferences . . . Somehow or other, though, Ernesto Durán has managed to get hold of that address and has started sending messages. When the first e-mail arrived, Karina immediately reported it to Dr Miranda. He read it and told her to ignore it and on no account to reply. She didn't even tell him about the second one, but although she said nothing to the doctor, she made a point of reading it herself. After that first e-mail, Karina, along with Adelaida, the receptionist working for the doctor next door, exchanged views on this very unusual patient. They had never come across anyone quite like Ernesto Durán. When the second e-mail arrived, they spent many hours discussing the case. Karina, who had seen Durán on two occasions, added a few physical details. She remembered him quite clearly as a thin, athletic-looking man. He was about thirty-five, with hair as dark as his eyes: asphalt black. He was attractive, but nothing special. He also had an inner strength, or so Karina felt, a sort of natural willpower that gave him a certain physical presence. Perhaps the only objectionable thing about him was his ears, which were, in Karina's view, too small. And Adelaida had added some comment like:

"I never trust men with small ears."

That is how Karina remembers him – neither pleasant nor unpleasant. The first time he visited the doctor, he had struck her as polite and friendly, but nothing more than that. He filled in his medical form and then sat down and waited. Karina was surprised when he didn't pick up a magazine as most patients do. Indeed, there are some people who *only* read in waiting rooms.

When he came for his second appointment, he seemed more nervous. Karina remembered clearly how he rested his hands on his knees, sighed and kept glancing around him, as if he couldn't control his eyes, or, rather, as if his face were obliged to follow them wherever they went. He also stood up several times and paced around, taking short steps. He went out into the corridor, then came back in, nodding briefly to her when he did. Then the telephone calls began. Ernesto Durán turned into a regular, repetitive irritant. Four or five out of every ten calls would have his voice at the other end. He was always cordial, polite, even affable, but then, one afternoon, Dr Miranda called her into his office and begged her, yes that was the word he used: "I beg you, please, Karina, not to put through any more calls from that patient," he said. "Not one. Never again. If he phones, I'm not in."

It wasn't easy. Durán was a persistent fellow, obsessed. It didn't take him long to realise that Karina had become a detour, and that their phone conversations were merely an eternal deferment. One day, he exploded. He felt humiliated, he'd had enough, it was a mockery, who did she think she was, he roared before slamming down the phone. Karina was left shaking. She managed to keep a grip on herself in front of the patients in the waiting room, but immediately got up and walked down the corridor to the toilet. While still managing to remain calm, she was nevertheless aware of the occasional internal shudder: Durán's shouts, or at least their echo, were in her body, trapped inside. When she looked at herself in the mirror, her eyes filled with tears. She felt ridiculous, furious, stupid. She washed her face, hoping to salvage a little of her pride from that cold water.

The following day, however, she was surprised to find a small box of chocolates and a little note waiting for her. Durán was asking her forgiveness. Half an hour later, he did so again over the phone. Karina treated him rather coolly, with a certain haughtiness in her curt, discreet replies, but it was clear that she was touched by the gesture. Durán, moreover, tried to go a little further, to put his case and explain his sense of urgency. Karina softened her tone somewhat and, in a spirit of camaraderie, explained that there was no point in making any further attempt to contact the doctor. She suggested an alternative strategy: when Dr Miranda was able to see him again, she herself would phone to arrange an appointment. When they said goodbye, neither of them felt much faith in the other. A whole week passed without a single "Hello" or "Good afternoon" from Ernesto Durán. Karina even came to the conclusion that he must finally have resigned himself to the situation. Then the first e-mail appeared. Then the second. Then the third. She read them all carefully. Although she was reluctant to admit it, she found them rather touching. She showed them to Adelaida, and they both agreed that Durán was clearly desperate and utterly sincere in what he wrote, that he was, in short, a sensitive man in difficulties. Adelaida even remarked that Dr Miranda's attitude seemed most unfair.

"Are you going to show him the latest e-mails?"

"Certainly not."

Karina knew her boss well. He had been absolutely clear on the matter: "If he phones, I'm not in."

Karina prints out the third e-mail and takes it with her to the small restaurant where the two friends have lunch together at least once a week. As well as the paella – which usually contains more onion and peppers than creatures of the sea – any new snippet of news from Durán always lights up the meal. They had both tried to imagine what life must be like for a man in the grip of such a vast, corrosive, potent fear. The two women felt moved when they read about the terrible sensations that assailed Durán whenever he felt he was about to faint. They also followed with great interest the tale of his failed encounter with the therapist Dr Miranda had recommended. But they want more. Adelaida wonders what he does for a job.

"He sounds to me like some sort of administrator."

"No, I don't think he's studied at all, he just works for the phone company as some kind of assistant."

Karina would also like to know more about his family life. When he got married and when he got divorced, for example. She finds it odd that he says nothing about his private life. What really happened with his ex-wife? Does he have a girlfriend now?

On this occasion, however, Karina seems less enthusiastic. She suspects that the new letter will answer none of these questions. Adelaida cannot contain her curiosity. Nor can she understand why the look on Karina's face has been one of fear and alarm ever since they set off for lunch together, ever since her friend announced the arrival of another e-mail.

"What's wrong? Tell me."

"I'm afraid, that's what's wrong."

"Why? What does the letter say?"

"I only read the first sentence."

"And one sentence was enough to give you a face like that?" asks Adelaida, astonished.

It isn't just fear that Karina feels, she feels disappointed too.

Up until now, Durán has been a gentle mystery, not threatening in the least. He could even be seen as picturesque or slightly eccentric, but never dangerous. The opening sentence of this third e-mail was a wake-up call, alarm bells had suddenly started ringing inside her. She felt unsure now; perhaps everything was far less romantic than she imagined. Perhaps Ernesto Durán wasn't just a lonely man with a fear of fainting and a desperate need to relate to someone. Perhaps he's a madman, someone with serious mental problems. Karina takes the letter out of her handbag and shows it to Adelaida.

"Read the opening sentence," she says, holding it out for her friend to see.

Dr Miranda,
I have a confession to make. I'm following you.

Andrés ought to go to his father, show him the X-rays, tell him the truth, tell him exactly what's happening; he should, moreover, explain that further tests are needed, that from now on, his relationship with medicine will become uncomfortably close, so close he'll grow to loathe it; he should go to his father and tell him that it's hopeless, that there's not a thing they can do about it, that he has cancer and doesn't have much longer to live. How long exactly? Medical calendars tend to be vague: not much longer. Which always means less.

But he doesn't do any of these things. Postponing duties, especially when those duties are painful ones, is also a temporary way of surviving. The poet William Carlos Williams was also a doctor. He wrote: "Many a time a man must watch the patient's mind as it watches him, distrusting him . . ." Andrés didn't know how his father would react when he found out the

43

truth. He distrusted both his and his father's minds because he wasn't at all sure about himself, about how he would react once he'd told his father the truth. He'd decided to confront the situation, however tragic, head on and talk to his father; but when the moment came, he didn't know how to, he felt invaded by thousands of tiny fears that raced around in his mind like trapped lizards and always led him to postpone that duty yet again: he should talk to his father, but not just then, later.

This morning, he again manages to distract himself from the task in hand. He has spent whole days using the same method. In order to ease his feelings of guilt, for he knows he doesn't have much time, he keeps himself busy with matters related to his father's illness, but which help him to avoid speaking to him directly. Now he's trying to negotiate with Merny. She's the woman who cleans Javier Miranda's apartment twice a week. On Thursdays, she does a thorough clean and on Tuesdays, she has just a quick tidy and then does any ironing. Andrés has left his father at the cinema with the children so that he can come and talk to her. He tells her everything, sparing her no detail, but warns that his father doesn't yet know, that he knows noth-ing. When Merny hears this, she seems slightly surprised, but she's never been one to show her feelings. She's a reserved woman. She doesn't ask many questions. Sometimes, it's not easy to guess what she's thinking, not, at least, for Andrés. When he suggests that she starts coming to the apartment every day, from Monday to Friday, Merny doesn't answer, she looks uncomfortable and eyes him rather warily. Andrés makes it clear that he's not asking her to be his father's nurse. He'll hire a nurse himself. He just wants her support, to know that she'll be there all the time to do the cooking every day and pop out to the pharmacy or the market if necessary. "What do you think,

Merny?" he asks.

She's thirty years old, a beautiful, dark-haired woman with ample hips and good legs. Her name, Merny, is a combination of two names. Her mother is called Mercedes and her father Nicolás. They put together the first syllables of their respective names to create a new one, Mer from Mercedes and Ni from Nicolás, Merni. It was the clerk at the registry office who made the "i" into a "y". Merny lives with a man called Jofre. Andrés has seen him a couple of times, but knows little about him. He knows he works as a bricklayer, but nothing more. Merny doesn't often talk about him either. She lives with him, but he isn't the father of her two sons; they're from her first man, a Colombian who went off to Barranquilla and never came back. Her oldest son is called Willmer and he's eleven years old. He's thin and gangly and is growing his hair long so that he can get some rasta braids. He likes rap and basketball. The youngest is called Yurber and he's only four. He's a chubby, smiley little fellow. In the morning, he goes to the school nearest where they live and in the afternoon, a girlfriend of Merny's looks after him. Willmer, on the other hand, is old enough to be out on the street by himself.

"The street's a dangerous place," says Merny. "There are a lot of bad people in the street. Just in the barrio next to ours you get kids of ten drinking and getting high on crack and carrying guns. Everyone knows about it, even the police, but they don't do anything. Perhaps just as well. They might make things worse." Then she adds: "Fortunately, Willmer's really into sport. So far, thank God, my son has turned out well."

Merny, Jofre, Willmer and Yurber. Andrés finds it odd that poor people should like such names. Why do they choose them? What's wrong with Juana or Gerardo? Why not Elena or

Luis or Inés or Ramón? Or do they perhaps find those names too ordinary, too dull and insipid, with no particular spark of their own? Perhaps that's why, when it comes to choosing a name, they turn to characters in films, baseball players, famous foreigners. Always in English, of course. He also doesn't understand parents who like to make up those strange combinations and burden their children with almost unpronounceable first names. That's very popular too. Like Merny. A son born to Jason and Mildred becomes Jamil. But then, when they go to the registry office, the same thing happens as happened with Merny. The clerk writes the name as he thinks fit: Yaimil. Yaimil Rodríguez. That's the name of one of the nurses who works nights at the hospital's A. & E. department. Other people might well think that it gets a child off to a bad start, that, for some, their first name is their very first disadvantage in life.

Merny doesn't see it like that. On the contrary. She's never said as much, but it's clear that she's proud of her sons' names. You could almost see it as an act of affirmation, a brief exercise of power, a victory. She has given birth to a child who will, no doubt, have a pretty hard time of it. Her baby is just another dot on the poverty line in the national statistics. Merny will probably have no control over anything. Hers is an existence bound to the state as regards health, education and work. Poverty seems to trace a path that always ends up in the state's apartments – be it bureaucracy or prison. Perhaps the only personal, private thing Merny could offer her children in that first moment was a name. A special name, a name like Willmer that has a ring of the future and of the north about it, something unusual. Or a different name, like Yurber, so different that only she could have thought of it. That perhaps is her personal seal, the one thing she can control, the surest thing she can give them. An illusion with a ring to it. The opportunity of a name.

Once, years ago, when she'd first started working for his father, Andrés had to drive her home. Someone called her from a public phone, from the barrio where she lives. Willmer would have been about nine months old. "Something's wrong," they said. "He's sick. You must come." Merny got very worried, but she looked at Andrés, taken aback, when he offered to give her a lift. He happened to be visiting his father that day. He even offered her medical help, but Merny refused. Almost reluctantly, she allowed him to take her in his car to a place near where she lived. They took the motorway, and she spoke very little, but kept restlessly moving in her seat, as if she had a strange ability to move her spinal column from one buttock to the other. And sometimes she waggled her fingers. Andrés tried to calm her and said again that if it was anything serious to please let him know. She asked him to drop her in the avenue at the foot of the hill, the vast mountain where the marginalised have slowly constructed their own difficult realm. There she would get a jeep that would take her a few miles further on, as far as a hill, near a police station, where she would get out and continue on foot up the concrete steps to her barrio, her house, and Willmer's fever.

It could take more than an hour. The last stretch alone consisted of more than four hundred steps. Her sister counted them once, she said, one by one, as she climbed them. She was coming back alone, at night. Four hundred and twenty-two steps to be exact. She did it to take her mind off feeling so frightened.

Andrés can vividly remember giving Merny that lift. It was at the height of the electoral campaign. On the way back home, he listened to the party political broadcasts on the radio. "The moment for the poor of this country has arrived," bawled one candidate, meanwhile inveighing against the old political parties and promising a new paradise. There's also a heaven where everyone is called Willmer.

Merny still lives in the same place and in the same way, with the same fears. How much time has she wasted going up and down those steps in order to come to his father's apartment? Twice a week every week. She comes to clean, to get rid of the dirt produced by someone else. Four hundred and twenty-two steps there and four hundred and twenty-two steps back. Plus the jeep, the avenue, the bus to the metro, twelve stations to another metro station, another avenue, and another bus to the door of the apartment building. It's a long way to come just to kneel down and get to grips with a stubborn stain between the tiles on the floor of a kitchen that isn't hers. Is that how she sees it? Is that how she feels? When she goes up the steps to her house, after a day's work. When she looks at that vast hill, crammed with tiny houses and hovels. Not even the police will venture into some of those barrios. When she goes up those steps and thinks that Willmer is no longer a baby with a fever, but that there are other dangers, like being old enough to kill someone. He could turn out to be a complete lout. What must she do to avoid that? How can she help him?

For a moment, Andrés wonders what lies behind Merny's look, behind those eyes which he sometimes finds elusive or even incomprehensible. What are they hiding? She's not happy with her life. How could she be? No-one could be happy with those four hundred and twenty-two steps. Is that what lies behind her look? Is that what lies behind her gaze? A dark, silent, long-repressed resentment? He suddenly feels cold. Perhaps Merny doesn't care about his father at all. She's spent years here, so close, so much part of their lives, but, at the same time, so far away. He looks at her now and feels that he doesn't know her, that he doesn't know what she thinks or feels about his father. Perhaps she's just thinking about her work. Perhaps, for her, the death of old Miranda is simply a work-related incident. Perhaps not. He's suddenly terrified by the thought that Merny might secretly hate them. Does she hate them?

At last, she speaks. She does so hesitantly, almost sadly, but without disguising what she feels, without hiding what she thinks. Merny doesn't like the idea of working for a man who is about to die. It's nothing personal, she just doesn't want to be in the apartment when, inevitably, Javier Miranda passes away. That, at any rate, is what Andrés deduces. She doesn't say as much, of course. She utters sighs more than words. She converses in vague sounds, interjections, thoughtful pauses. In the end, she says that she'll think about it. That's all. She'll think about it.

"I'll tell you later. Now I've got to finish cleaning the bathroom."

Dear Dr Miranda,
I have a confession to make: I'm following you. I'd love to see your face now, to see your reaction. What do you think? Does it bother you? Does it worry you? Does it frighten you perhaps? Or maybe you don't even care, perhaps you even find it amusing. I no longer know what to think. Let me just make it clear that I haven't begun following you because I want to, but out of sheer desperation. I've tried everything, but you don't answer my e-mails, your secretary lies to me, and I don't know how else to get you to listen to me, to resolve my situation.

Now I think that perhaps this is the only way to make you understand how hounded I feel, how all this is affecting me. I'm even starting to have problems at work. I'm beginning to think they might fire me. I mean it. The attacks are getting ever more frequent, and every time that I feel I'm about to faint, and my blood pressure plummets, I usually try and get to the toilets quickly. I splash my face with cold water and breathe deeply. Sometimes, too, I do a quick handstand, like we used to in gym lessons at school. I support myself on my hands and rest my feet against the wall. That way the blood flows back into my head and I know then I won't faint.

A little while ago, a supervisor came up to me with a strange smile on his face and said that a rumour was going around that, lately, I spend most of my time in the toilets. Another day, I was doing a handstand, as I've explained, and a colleague from the next office came in. Needless to say, he was very surprised to find me there like that. I tried to explain the situation to him, but I'm sure he didn't believe me. Perhaps he thought I was mad. The truth is I feel more and more uncomfortable at work. I can tell they're talking about me, and they look at me suspiciously. I know that when they see me, they nudge each other and whisper.

The day before yesterday, Doctor, I could bear it no longer. I took advantage of the fact that the office was being fumigated and left early to look for you. I know you only see patients from three o'clock in the afternoon, but I thought perhaps you might be engaged on some other activity at the hospital. I thought you might be visiting your patients or performing an operation. I wandered about all over the place, I even went to the coffee bar. I also asked a couple of nurses if they'd seen you. I didn't find you, but I have to say that just being there, looking for you, made me feel better.

Then, just when I was about to come home, I spotted you in the distance, on the ground floor. I was walking along and there you were at the far end of the corridor, about to get into one of the lifts that go down to the car park. I walked as fast as I could to try and reach you, but I was too slow. By the time I got there, the lift doors had closed. I felt quite desperate then. And I raced for the stairs, the way people do in films. I tore down them, I even bumped into a lady with a walking stick, but carried on regardless. It was almost a race against the clock: as you know, there are five levels in the underground car park. How could I possibly know where you'd parked your car? How could I possibly know at which level you would get out of the lift? That's why I ran down the stairs, almost two at a time, peering in at every level, trying to catch you, trying to see if I might spot you. You were wearing a pale green shirt and blue trousers.

I didn't find you. I never saw you. I reached level 5 gasping for breath. The lift doors opened and out came a woman carrying a little girl in her arms. The child had her head in bandages and was very pale. Her lips looked as if they had been painted green. When she saw me, the woman took fright and hurried off to where the cars were parked. I stayed there for a while to get my breath back. Then I started thinking about what would have happened if I'd managed to catch you up. How would you have reacted? Would you have recognised me at once? Would you know who I was?

I spent the afternoon feeling oddly relieved. Perhaps it's the same relief I feel when I send you these letters.

Knowing that we're sure to meet again soon,

Ernesto Durán

He takes the afternoon off. He phones his secretary and cancels all his appointments. Then he goes to Maripérez station and gets the cable car. It's a weekday, so he doesn't have to wait long. The only other people in the queue are some boys, playing truant, escaping from that organised tedium known as secondary school. They spend the whole ride laughing and joking. Andrés says nothing. One of his own kids might bunk off school one Wednesday to form part of just such a group. They guffaw loudly. One of them has bought a pack of cigarettes. They're probably planning to smoke them on top of El Ávila. They're about thirteen or fourteen. Andrés considers talking to them, telling them he's a doctor, warning them about the dangers of smoking. Smoking kills, even when you're only fifteen, he could say. But he doesn't. There's no point. He was that age once, he's been there. Adolescence is the most unclassifiable of joys.

It's been far too long since Andrés has been up to the top of that mountain. There was a time, in his youth, when he would come whenever he could. El Ávila was like nature's shopping mall, with few if any regulations, and instead of shop windows, there were dark, mysterious corridors full of nettles, lots of paths you could get lost down. Andrés and Vicente, his best friend at the time, used to go there every week. They even made the climb on foot sometimes. They could take any route: La Julia, Quebrada Pajaritos, Cotiza, even, when they were feeling really adventurous, reaching the peak of Naiguatá, the highest point on the coastal mountain range. They used to sit there on a huge rock. If there were no clouds, you could see the city of Caracas on one side and the sea on the other. They would sit there talking nonsense and smoking marijuana. This was no mere diversion for Vicente, a weekend spliff; he devoted himself with real seriousness to organising this ritual. He took almost a professional pride in it. He used to get hold of all kinds of different stuff. Once, he turned up with some really high-quality Jamaican weed. They smoked their respective joints and stretched out on the rocks, gazing up at the sky. They spent hours like that, not even talking, a faint, foolish smile on their lips.

The light is whiter up there. The sun is like a slap in the face. It burns differently, it spreads itself, as if it, too, were lying stretched out in the upper air. The wind cuts your lips. Its fingers are like razor blades. They didn't so much climb the mountain as float on it.

The last he heard of Vicente was that he was living near Tampa, Florida, selling vacuum cleaners. It didn't seem possible that the university timetable could have put asunder what marijuana had so forcefully joined together. Vicente was the brother Andrés never had. When Andrés began studying medicine, Vicente had just started his degree in engineering. They simply stopped seeing each other, and the process seemed so natural that it even occurred to Andrés that their friendship had merely been another subject on the secondary school curriculum. Just as he had got through maths, through the indescribable tedium of Spanish and the apathy of history, so he had got through his friendship with Vicente. Years later, while queuing up to see a film, he met one of his erstwhile friend's brothers, who told him that Vicente had moved to the States, where he lived a comfortable enough life, an Electrolux life, with his wife and three kids.

From the Hotel Humboldt, near the cable-car station, you can't see the city and the sea at the same time simply by turning your head. There are no enormous rocks and not even the sun seems quite so close. Andrés takes his nostalgia for a walk. Even at that age, when he wasn't yet fifteen, he dreamed of becoming a doctor. If he were asked to say precisely when and how he decided to study medicine, he would have to think about it for a long time. People see sickness as a definitive sign: the body within the body, a sign that is at once troubling and disgusting. Perhaps that's why it's usually assumed that medicine is a stubborn, obstinate vocation, almost genetic in its purity: you're born a doctor, born without a fear of peering into other people's bodies and with strength enough to cast an unflinching eye upon other people's blood.

Andrés, however, doesn't feel this is so in his case. He thinks that, for him, medicine was, at first, born more out of curiosity than out of a sense of vocation. He's never believed that being a doctor is a variant of being a missionary, an almost religious calling, a kind of voluntary service based on a charitable impulse or on the ideal of spending one's life saving other people. Medicine isn't a human quality, it isn't a virtue.

When he scrutinises his memory, he always bumps up against the same image: one morning, very early, on El Agua beach, on Isla Margarita. Andrés would have been ten years old, and his mother had just died. Perhaps that's why his father decided that the two of them should go and spend a week on the island. They travelled by ferry, naturally. It was part of a family plan to dismantle the apartment in Caracas and cleanse it of any hint of his mother's presence, so as to spare him further traumas. His father took him to the beach while his sisters-in-law checked the shelves, shared out the clothes, the jewellery and any other belongings that had survived the fatal air crash. On their return, he and his father would find a place with less of a past. The void was preferable. It would be less painful.

They caught the ferry in Puerto La Cruz. It was a noisy old boat. Andrés felt as if he were boarding a rusty whale. It was a real adventure. He ran about on the deck, spent hours watching the sea, waiting for the dolphins to appear, leaping among the waves. He had never been on a ferry before. He had never been on an island. When he remembers it now, he thinks how terrible those same moments must have been for his father. There is Javier Miranda, widower, and his ten-year-old son.

"Come on," he keeps saying. "What do you want to do next?"

He shows him the sea, points at the curling waves, remains watching by his side, waiting for surprising animals to emerge from the water. There he is, doing everything he can to make his son forget, to stop him missing his mother, to fill up his mother's absence with sun and salt water. The Caribbean is trying to conspire against Freud. Andrés runs to and fro while his father grants his every whim, buys him an orange drink, buys him a fish pasty; when, at last, they spy the coast of the island, the port of Punta de Piedras, they both lean on the rail to witness that encounter with the land. His father tells him about the beaches that await them, of the marvellous time they're going to have. That was his way of mourning: organising a party for his son.

Over the years, Andrés had gradually managed to track down his first flicker of interest in medicine to that time, to that week on Isla Margarita. It happened on the third day. His father always got him up very early, as if he were afraid that Andrés might wake alone, as if he didn't want him to have a moment without some stimulus, some distraction. As soon as the sun rose, his father would get him out of bed, always eager to invent some new surprise, some new adventure. The previous day they had gone fishing, without success. That morning he proposed running down to the beach to look for jellyfish. At that hour, when the light was still weak and the sand cold, they would be sure to find a few lost among the last fingers of the waves. Some of those white medusas, which could sting you when in the water, always got washed up on the shore during the night. The less cautious, the less experienced, the fat and the flabby, didn't make it back, but remained there on the sand, along with other detritus from the sea, condemned to a slow death, drying up and suffocating in the air and the sun.

Andrés only woke properly when the icy water touched his feet. They walked for nearly half a mile but found only one small jellyfish. However, parked on the sand at the end of the beach was a police car. Next to it stood a group of officers. He and his father ran towards them. A man's body lay on the sand. His clothes were slightly tattered, his skin purple and his lips very swollen. Out of the cavity of his right eye sprouted some yellow foam, like very pale broccoli, like some sort of soft coral emerging from the man's head. Javier Miranda squeezed his son's arm and tried to drag him away, but Andrés stayed where he was, absorbed, studying the body. The policemen gave some vague explanation. The man wasn't a tourist. They assumed he was a local fisherman. They were waiting for a pathologist to arrive and examine the body.

"He's alive!" said Andrés in an anxious, childish voice.

While his father was listening to what the policemen had to say, Andrés, intrigued, had gone closer to the body. He heard it breathe. He saw the gaping mouth, saw the fat lips tremble slightly; he crouched down and once more heard the man breathe.

"He's alive!" he said again, shouting this time.

Only his father hurried over to him and took his hand. The officers looked at each other and smiled. One of them laughed out loud. Or that, at least, is what Andrés remembers.

"He's breathing," he murmured rather sadly, while his father drew him away from the corpse.

"No, he's not," said the policeman. "Listen, kid. What you can hear is the water moving around inside the body. That's all. Listen," he repeated, crouching down beside him. They all stayed still for a moment in expectation, and a liquid whisper slipped out onto the air. "Did you hear that? It's just water. But the guy's dead alright."

Andrés was astonished. He imagined that body full of sea, full of water that came and went, that made noises, that went round and round, unable to escape. He thought of it as a secret room, in which the water could circulate freely. That morning, Andrés thinks, marked his initial curiosity about bodies, the discovery of the existence of an order distinct from words, more physical, more tactile, less invisible. His father had to drag him away. The boy wanted to wait for the pathologist to come, he wanted to know what would happen next. His father, of course, feared that the incident would lay bare the very loss he was trying to conceal. One death calls to another. A stranger's body lying on the sand was also the body of the mother, floating and turning between them, surrounding them, drenching them.

Andrés cannot remember there being any further consequences. He can't, for example, remember if it was that same day that he spoke with his father about the death, about the plane exploding in mid-air; he can't remember if his recurring dream came before or after that morning spent hunting for jellyfish on the beach. He merely pinpoints that moment, almost fancifully, as a first image of his vocation. At seventeen, when he finished secondary school, he decided to study medicine – in a rather childish way, as is always the case at that age – and he still felt driven by that same curiosity, by the desire to find out what went on inside our bodies.

It's seven o'clock when he comes down from the mountain. There's no-one else in the cable car. He feels that chance has handed him a rare privilege. The journey back to the city reveals an extraordinary landscape. The illuminated lines of the motorways, the lights of the suburbs and the barrios, draw a different map in the darkness, that of an unfamiliar, almost unreal city: a stationary landscape, bereft of movement, a Caracas conjured up in that very moment that will surely disappear as soon as he enters it again. Suspended in the air, almost hanging above the distant precipice that is now the city, Andrés makes a decision, rings his father's number from his mobile and says:

"Hi, Dad. How do you fancy coming to Isla Margarita with me?"

In its heyday, the bar had been an old-fashioned Spanish *tasca*. Legs of serrano ham hung from the walls and customers were always offered a little snack, a *tapa*, with their drink – some bread and a sliver of potato omelette, a few grilled sardines, some olives. Now, all that's left of that Spanish heritage is its name: Las Cibeles. It's just a bar where the people who work locally take refuge after six o'clock. Office workers, secretaries, administrators and low-grade civil servants meet up to exchange the gossip of the day with the help of a few beers. The whole place is filled with a beery torpor, a chemical smell that even indicates the way to the toilets. At one end of the bar, Adelaida and Karina have had to wait until evening to finish their after-lunch conversation. Ernesto Durán's latest letter remains the juiciest dish on the menu.

"I couldn't say anything to Dr Miranda because he rang in early and said he was cancelling all his appointments. He said he wouldn't be coming in this afternoon. As you know, he's worried about his father, who's in a really bad way apparently."

Adelaida barely has time to nod. Karina seems so resolute, she's speaking very rapidly and with great determination. She has thought of nothing else all afternoon.

"This has gone too far," she says now, nervously smoothing her blouse. "If not today, then I'll have to do it tomorrow, because this is something I really must tell the doctor about."

"There's no need to make such a drama out of it, Karina. It's hardly the end of the world."

"But what if the guy really is mad?" asks Karina, genuinely concerned.

"He only followed him once, for one morning. He's desperate. He needs to see his doctor."

"Please, Adelaida, I'm being serious."

"So am I." She gives her friend a sly look, shifts closer to her and says softly: "We've all done crazy things in our time. Do you remember when I asked you to come with me to follow Cheo, and how we ended up in that awful place on Avenida Lecuna?"

"Yes, you wanted to find out if he really was playing dominoes with his friends!" says Karina. Adelaida nods sagely and flings her arms wide as if to underline the absurdity of the whole experience.

"Well, wasn't *that* a mad thing to do?"

"God, yes, it was real dive, full of whores and drunks," says Karina. "You had a kind of hunch that he was two-timing you, cheating on you, but you needed proof."

"If anyone had seen the two of us there, at that moment, at that hour of night, in that place, tailing my husband and trying to catch him out, what would they have thought of us, what would they have said?"

They look at each other for a second. Is this what's happening to Ernesto Durán? Does he need proof and is he trying, however ineptly, to find that proof as best – or worst – as he can? He doesn't care, he's lost control. As we all do sometimes, as anyone can: it's not so very hard to lose control; it happens when you least expect it. Just as Adelaida had had her suspicions and needed some evidence to back them up, so too, perhaps, Durán feels the same need to find out the truth, which is what he's trying to do. He can't go on living without knowing what's really wrong with him. Sickness is a form of disloyalty, an unacceptable infidelity.

By the time she's on her third beer, Adelaida has an idea.

"And what if *you* answered the letter?"

"*What?*"

"Why don't you write to him as if you were Dr Miranda?"

"You must be out of your mind, Adelaida! How could you even think of such a thing?"

"What's wrong with the idea?"

"Everything. Dr Miranda is Dr Miranda and Karina Sánchez is Karina Sánchez. Besides, you can't just play a trick like that, you—"

"Wait, wait. Listen." Adelaida interrupts her and moves her stool closer. "Just think about it for a second. If you tell Dr Miranda everything, if you show him this e-mail, what do you think will happen?"

Karina hesitates for a moment. She imagines Andrés, grave-faced, standing before her, holding the printed e-mail in his hands, reading it. But the scene dissolves at once, it goes no further.

"I don't know. I haven't a clue. He could react in all kinds of ways."

"Exactly." Adelaida draws still closer. "He might laugh it off and do nothing at all. Or he might phone the police. He could get this Durán guy into a lot of trouble."

"But—"

"Wait, I haven't finished. Look, I'm not suggesting you commit a crime, Karina. You know the doctor well, don't you? How long have you been working for him now?"

"Seven years."

"Longer than many marriages. Right then: you know his style, know more or less how he writes and what he might say to a patient like Durán."

"But I'm not a doctor. I've never studied medicine."

"That doesn't matter. All that matters is that you write to him, that you reply."

"You don't know what you're saying."

"Of course I do. I think what that man needs is for someone to speak nicely to him, to listen to him, to give him a little atten-tion."

"And I think the beer is going to your head, Adelaida."

"Just try it. Write to him once. Even if only to make him stop following the doctor, so that he has one less thing to worry about. That way, you'll be helping them both."

Karina again hesitates for a second, a second into which all her questions fit and into which slips the possibility that, yes,

61

she really could do it. All temptations rely on such seconds. It's all they need.

"What have you got to lose?"

The truth is she has nothing to gain either. But the temptation is still there, waiting for her. Why? Is it that she fancies Ernesto Durán? That first time, when she saw him come into the office, she had perhaps liked the look of him, but there had been no chemical charge, she hadn't felt an immediate, unnameable attraction. Durán first began to touch her heart with his e-mails. She has got to know him more from having read those than from having seen or spoken to him. Through writing and reading she has begun to develop a kind of melancholic complicity that was now becoming a tension, a risk. The man behind the words interested her more than the man she'd seen or with whom she'd spoken on the phone. It was as if they were two different men, and she didn't yet know which was more real, more authentic. Was that what tempted her?

"Alright," said Karina, with a faint smile. "I'll do it once. Just once."

Dear Señor Durán,

I must, first of all, apologise that it has taken me so long to respond to your e-mails. The life of a doctor is an extremely busy one, as you know, and these last few weeks have been particularly hectic.

I have read carefully what you had to say and found it most interesting. For the moment, I think that you must try to remain calm and, above all, do nothing foolish. By which I mean, of course, following me. I have nothing against you, and I intend to keep a close eye on your case and, as soon as I can, will attend to you personally.

I will be away at a conference outside the city this week, but, the moment I return, I will be in touch with you again. Meanwhile, if it affords you some help and relief, feel free to continue writing to me.

Hoping that this letter restores to you a little much-needed calm, I remain,

Yours sincerely,

Andrés Miranda

When Andrés told Karina that he would be taking a few days' holiday on Isla Margarita with his father, she saw in this the hand of God, and sensed behind or beneath this unusual turn of events the invisible fingers of a far superior force. Her boss' sudden absence also proved to be her muse and gave her the push she needed to reply to Durán's letter. It took her a while. She tried to put herself in the doctor's place, she experimented with various tones and wrote several rough drafts before arriving at the definitive version. In the past, Dr Miranda had asked her to write the occasional short message, usually in response to the sales departments of pharmaceutical companies. These had been concise letters of only a few lines, in which she had politely thanked the sales people for certain medical samples they'd sent, but never anything memorable or personal, and certainly nothing that presented her with a stylistic challenge that sent a shiver of excitement through her, the fascinating twinge of anxiety she felt when confronted by the blank computer screen: being able to choose had aroused in her an indescribable sensation, a kind of thrilling void in her mind. She felt she was as likely to sit paralysed for a few seconds as to feel an urgent, unstoppable need to write a stream of words, extravagant and uncontrollable. Being able to choose, for example, which word to use for "Dear" – *Estimado* or *Apreciado* – was a revelation to her. Karina spent almost an hour turning over each word, savouring the sharpness of the consonants, the rotundity of certain vowels, weighing up the effect that each might have on Durán. It was no small matter: it was, after all, the first word that Dr Miranda had addressed to him in a long time. In the end, she opted for *Estimado*, partly because it seemed to her more formal, more cautious, and partly, too, because she liked the *e*. However hard she tried, she could find no other reason, no other cause. She simply liked beginning the letter with an *e*. And that was that.

As regards his other patients, Andrés had spoken to Miguel, who promised to attend to them in case of emergency. Maricruz Fernández, another doctor at the hospital, had also undertaken to step in if necessary. He met with no objections from his family either: Mariana thought it an excellent idea, and the children, after some initial resistance, soon had to admit defeat: their father and grandfather would be travelling during the week, and the children couldn't possibly miss school. His father was somewhat suspicious at first, but Andrés soon clarified any doubts he might have by saying that the trip was strictly a business matter: a company on the verge of bankruptcy was offering him a house in lieu of payment, and, thinking it might be a good investment, he'd decided to go and take a look at it, and then remembering the journey they'd made there together all those years before, he'd thought: why not repeat the experience?

Now he's on the deck of the ferry looking back at the port. It's so similar and so different from the image of himself in that same place and in that same position all those years ago. He has a faint smile on his lips. He's amused by his own silliness, by the childish ploy of inventing a house and a bankrupt company; there's something about the lie that delights him: it's the blithe uncertainty, the not knowing how or when he will continue the lie or make it real or where he will find such a house, and just how he will disentangle himself from the fantasy that is serving as the reason for the trip. Andrés rests both arms on the ship's rail and watches as the port of La Guaira grows gradually smaller. The horizon is the only reliable measure of speed, and that horizon, growing ever more blurred and diffuse, is the only sign of reality he now has. The boat is too large a piece of machinery for him to be able to tell whether it's really moving or not, or if, like a dog, dizzy with salt and seawater, its going round and round in circles on the waves. Only the horizon changes, by disappearing.

"What are you thinking about?" His father has come back from the toilets and joins him at the rail.

"Oh, nothing. I was just looking at the sea. Would you like a beer?"

His father says he would and they both make their way to the bar. The ferry is almost empty, apart from a few German tourists, who always look slightly lost, as if someone had tricked them, as if Venezuela were a geographical error, a mistake in their Berlin travel agent's leaflet. One of the tables inside is occupied by a man and a woman. Andrés had noticed them when they boarded the ferry. She is a good-looking mulatta of about thirty, with straight hair and a slightly sad expression. She's wearing a pair of beige shorts and a white sleeveless T-shirt that barely contains her small, firm breasts. The man is a classic fat guy, with the typical belly of a forty-something male who spends more time drinking beer than doing sit-ups. In fact, he's drinking a beer right now. He's also glued to his mobile phone and talking in a very loud voice, moving about in his chair, making grandiloquent gestures, and looking scornfully at the woman, as if she were a nuisance, as if being with her were a tiresome duty. His attitude is so blatant that Andrés begins to wonder if he's actually talking to anyone. He speaks so loudly, issuing orders and instructions, as if he were addressing employees, mere subalterns. He never receives any calls. As soon as he ends one call, he immediately dials another number and recommences his brief routine: he gets to his feet, paces up and down, beating the air with one hand, projecting his voice and generally strutting about, with the clear intention of being noticed and heard by other people. He shows no hint of embarrassment and never lowers his voice. Andrés concludes that the whole thing is an act, an act that the woman finds harder and harder to bear, which is why she has that melancholy look tattooed on her face; she clearly does feel embarrassed and probably thinks this must be obvious to anyone. Perhaps she's thinking that her husband, boyfriend, partner or whatever is making a complete fool of himself. At one point, when he's some distance away, he shouts something to her that Andrés doesn't quite catch, and then he realises that the fat guy has ordered her to go and buy him another beer. He's gripping his mobile in his right hand and the empty can in his left. The mobile phone survives, but the can is crushed, crumpled and hurled into the sea.

"Do you mind having to travel by ferry?"

His father feels guilty: the only reason they're on this five-hour boat trip is because of him and his phobias. If he wasn't still so afraid of flying, they could have made the same journey by plane, gliding through the air for a mere thirty minutes.

Andrés tells him it doesn't matter, it's fine, they're in no hurry, besides, he's enjoying being back on a ferry. Javier Miranda isn't so sure and thinks his son is just saying this to keep him quiet. Not that he minds; in fact, he's very grateful. His fear of flying is far greater than any other fear. He can't control it. He feels that he couldn't even step onto a landing strip without trembling. He imagines he would turn blue, that his lips would swell up and he'd feel a sharp pain in his cheekbones, as if his eyes were trying to escape into his body. The mere image of a plane in the air is enough to make him feel sick. He needs to think about something else.

"The last time we made this trip, your mother had just died," he says.

"Yes, I know. You wanted to take my mind off things," replies Andrés. "You wanted to get me out of the apartment. That's why we came."

Then Javier thinks that perhaps they're doing the same again, only in reverse. It takes him a while to unravel that sentence, although he understood it perfectly well when he thought it: they're making the same journey, but this time, perhaps it's Andrés, his son, who's trying to take *his* mind off things. Can this be true? It's a question he doesn't dare ask himself.

When they can just make out the port of Punta de Piedras, when it's still only a smudge of shadow sewn onto the bottom of the sky, the fat guy asks the woman to get him another beer. Now everyone is out on deck. Most of the few passengers gather at the front of the boat and watch the coast, their next fixed destination, coming nearer. A boy is shouting insistently at the sea, the same word over and over: dolphins! He elongates the vowels, stretches them out until they squeak: Dooolphiiins! And then he whistles to them. Perhaps someone has told him that dolphins are like dogs. At any rate, the boy shouts at them as if he believed they were. He shouts at his parents too, protesting, complaining that during the whole trip, they haven't seen a single memorable sea creature. Not a whale, not a tuna, not a dolphin.

"You lied to me!" he screams.

His parents look thoroughly fed up and, as if their son were the responsibility of the other passengers, go back inside, leaving the child on deck.

"We'll be right back, Roberto," they say.

"Dooolphiiins!"

Andrés goes inside too. The truth is he's intrigued by the woman with the fat guy. On the pretext of getting a coffee, he heads towards the covered part of the boat. His father stays outside, staring at the horizon, at the fringe of land that is still no more than a mist, a distant stain. The interior of the boat is air-conditioned, but it still doesn't make things very cool, or at least not cool enough. There are flies as well, buzzing unsteadily about, almost as if they were giddy; they drift drowsily around in the middle of the room. It occurs to Andrés that the boy on deck would be better off looking for flies rather than dolphins. But he forgets the thought at once when he approaches the bar where the woman is waiting for the beer she's ordered. He leans on the bar next to her and smiles, trying to be friendly. He's suddenly filled by a sense of the ridiculous: how many years has it been since he did something like this? He doesn't want to seduce the woman, simply to play at seducing her, to flex his flirting muscles and return to a gym he hasn't visited in a long time. The woman smiles back. It seems to Andrés, however, that the smile is just a smile, and so he says nothing. A few seconds pass, then Andrés gives a half-yawn, a fairly bad imitation, but he can't do any better, and he smiles again. He orders a coffee. He waits a few seconds more, looking at the woman out of the corner of his eye before attempting to start a conversation:

"It drags a bit, doesn't it?" he says, but immediately regrets having said this. "It drags a bit." What does that mean exactly?

"Yes, it does," she replies, after a pause.

Andrés gives her a broad, grateful smile. Her smile is rather less broad, but he doesn't mind. The barman returns with the beer, and the woman pays. Andrés asks if she lives on Isla Margarita, but she says, no, she lives in Maracay, she's with her husband, who has come to the island on business. Andrés understands then that the fat guy speaking interminably into his phone to no-one at all is, first, her husband, and second, a man who does deals and goes on business trips. The woman doesn't leave. She appears to be waiting for his coffee to arrive. She doesn't seem particularly bothered about taking her husband's drink to him as quickly as possible. Secretly, it pleases Andrés to think of the beer getting warm. They begin a desultory conversation, as if led on by natural curiosity, as if the only thing that has brought them together is the implacable need to kill time. Thus he learns that her name is Yadira, that she does little else but be the fat guy's woman, that she's not married to him, although she calls him her husband, that they have no children, and it remains unclear whether they live together or if Yadira is his second front, the branch office of the fat guy's proper family. Andrés lies and says he's divorced and is going with his father to spend a few days at the beach: it's sometimes good to get a change of air, he says. He's not quite clear why he's saying all this, but feels it's part of the game, that this is how he's expected to behave. He orders another coffee. She continues to talk about her life, more cheerfully now, offering more details.

The can of beer sits sweating on the bar.

Yadira is talking about her adolescence, telling him why she left school, when, suddenly, the fat guy with the mobile phone appears, his face pressed to the fibre-glass window, where he's watching them from outside, from the deck. He raps with his knuckles on the opaque plastic, his squashed nose looking even more like a snout. He's obviously not at all pleased. Yadira doesn't even say goodbye. She picks up the can and leaves.

"Where did you go to buy the coffee? Caracas?" his father asks.

"I got chatting to a girl," Andrés says, smiling and proffering the small disposable cup. His father takes a sip and scans the deck, as if trying to locate which girl had kept his son talking.

"That one." Andrés saves him the trouble and points at the fat guy, who is no longer issuing instructions down his mobile phone, but is clearly telling Yadira off.

"She's pretty," Javier says.

Andrés nods. Then they turn back to the island. Now it really is an island; they can make out its shape and texture, the yellowish-red colour of the parched earth. The glare of the sun burns their eyes. Then his father, by various circuitous routes, tries to find out if there's some special reason for the journey they're making. Andrés senses at once what his father is after and realises that behind all his father's words lie the clinical tests, the C.T. scan, the results from the M.R.I. scan … There they all are in the middle of the sea. There, too, are an operating theatre, catheters snaking through the water, drifting gauze, tubes, bits of paper, syringes. The sun is a yellow stethoscope. Andrés snatches a sideways glance at his father, using his right hand clamped to his eyebrows as a sun visor. This could be a good moment to tell him the truth. Is it? Is it a good moment?

Isn't it perhaps too soon? They haven't even reached the island yet. What would happen then? What would the trip be like once Andrés has told him the truth?

"I don't know," his father says, trying to bring what he's trying to ask to a close. "I just thought there might be something else, you know what I mean."

There is always something else. Something that moves and hurts and no longer works. That is the inevitable story of bodies, the biography of deterioration. Health is an immutable ideal. The most perverse of all utopias. Michel Foucault said that, viewed from the experience of death, illness can even be seen as a function of life. "Paradoxically, from the corpse's point of view, it looks like life." Exactly. Health doesn't exist, it's a heaven that forms no part of existence: we human beings can only live while sick. It's just that in his father's case, the illness is in its final stages. What comes after that? His father is still looking at him, as if secretly he, too, was awaiting that revelation. Why doesn't he tell him the truth now, this instant?

Yadira's scream is like a blow with a stone. Everyone spins round: she's not actually lying on the ground, but that's only because the fat guy has hold of her by the hand. He has just punched her in the face. Yadira is shielding her face and shaking her head.

"Let me go!" she howls.

The only response from the fat man is to give her a kick. Then another, in her belly or higher up. He may have struck her ribs or her breasts. Andrés tries to rush to her aid, but his father holds him back. "Don't be a fool," he says. "Don't get involved."

His father is so tense that his nails dig into his son's body. The other onlookers cry out; the German tourists watch, not entirely clear if what they are seeing is real or part of some picturesque welcome ceremony; two of the crew members run towards the couple and try to intervene, but not before the fat man has slapped Yadira so hard that this time he floors her. When they grab hold of him, he continues to struggle and roar, heaping insults on her. Another two members of the crew arrive and carry him, struggling, away. Yadira remains alone for a few seconds, sitting on the deck, shrunk in upon herself. Head bowed, she covers her face, and sobs, like a small wounded, frightened animal. Andrés tries again to go over to her, but his father, with surprising force, stops him.

"No, don't you go," he says quietly. "Not unless you want her to get an even worse beating."

Andrés looks at him in surprise. A woman goes to Yadira and helps her up, giving her a handkerchief to wipe away the blood on her face. As Yadira walks towards the toilets, she briefly catches Andrés' eye and immediately looks away.

As they drive off the ferry, they pass the couple. Yadira still has her eyes fixed on the ground, and beside her is the fat man, talking on his mobile phone, while a driver loads their suitcases into the boot of a taxi. Then the driver opens the car door, and the fat man stands to one side, still talking, so that Yadira can get into the car first. When she does, he roughly strokes her hair, and she, rather unconvincingly, avoids his touch. During the whole journey to the hotel, Andrés keeps looking at the taxi in his rear-view mirror. At one point, on the motorway, the evening light transforms the taxi into a razor blade, a slender metal blade following them, unhurriedly, always keeping the same distance, the same speed, always there, always sharp, always following them. Andrés looks at his father sitting next to him, overcome by sleep, no longer asking any questions.

Sunk in sleep, he seems happier, he seems safe.

Dear Dr Miranda,

You answered me! I still can't believe it! I swear that as soon as I saw your name in my in-box, I froze. My eyes filled with tears, I mean it. I got up, I took a few steps, sat down again, got up, sat down . . . I didn't know what to do. I felt like shouting, jumping, running. I wanted to go out and ring the neighbours' doorbells or rush to the window and shout: He wrote to me! Dr Miranda has finally written to me! My eyes filled with tears, Doctor, they really did. In fact, to be honest, they're still full of tears. I think that I'm too shocked right now to be able to answer. I just wanted to say thank you, Doctor. Thank you! Thank you! Thank you!

Ernesto Durán

Dear Dr Miranda,

I've just sent you an e-mail that I now wish I could erase. It suddenly occurred to me that I may have come across as too effusive, a bit crazy. Please don't be alarmed. It was just the reaction of the moment. Please don't be frightened. It really was a momentary madness because I felt so pleased and happy. I do hope you understand. I wouldn't want to scare you off again.

Yours sincerely,

Ernesto Durán

Dear Dr Miranda,

Just one more thing. I thought of it after I'd sent you the previous message. But once you've sent a message, you've sent it. There's no getting it back. Then I thought of other things as well. And I wanted to say that, from now on, *you* set the rules. I wanted you to know that I'm ready to do whatever you say, that, from now on, our relationship will be entirely on your terms. You are the doctor, after all. I promise you I've changed. I promise that I'm already much better.

Yours gratefully,
Ernesto Durán

The days they spend on the island are not as Andrés expected, starting with the scenery: there's nothing about the beach or the sea that reminds him of the island of his childhood. It seems bizarre to think that once, early in the morning, the beach was full of dead jellyfish; now, each morning, it's full of German and Canadian tourists, hefty men with tattoos on their arms, terribly pale-skinned people who perhaps run a petrol station in Hamburg and are now taking advantage of a cheap holiday in the Caribbean. However, this is just a detail, a daily excuse not to face up to what he's come there to do. It doesn't matter which beaches they go to, what plans they make, he still cannot speak to his father. He watches the hours and the scenery pass with the same feeling of impotence, incapable of telling him the truth.

One day, they go to Macanao, the wildest, remotest part of the island, where the sun appears to have got stuck, its gaze fixed for ever on one stone. The light is very low. The desert landscape is another version of the sea, with which it contrasts or converses. They are two parts of the same body, the blue sea that seems to move as naturally as breathing and the brown earth, eternally motionless. Not even there, on Playa de Punta

Arena, can Andrés confront his father and tell him once and for all the terrible news. He can never find the appropriate moment, there's always something not quite right, he can never get up the courage. He starts to think then that the trip wasn't a good idea, that it takes more than just a change of location to be able to speak the truth. The sea and the earth, blue and brown, seem to him parts of the same cadaver.

He finds it very hard to get to sleep at night, and when he does finally manage it, he sleeps badly, fitfully. He never feels rested when he wakes up; he gets out of bed like someone coming home from a dark and arduous task, as if returning to the light after a fierce battle. When he opens his eyes each morning, he feels that he's in flight from something, that he's escaped by the skin of his teeth, who knows from what, who knows how? He doesn't even remember what it was he was dreaming; he just has a feeling of dense anxiety beneath his eyelids, nothing more.

His father, on the other hand, seems to sleep peacefully. Andrés would have preferred not to share a double room, but his father insisted, it seemed to him an unnecessary expense to have a room each.

"After all, we are family," he muttered to the clerk who greeted them at the hotel reception.

That's doubtless what family is for, thought Andrés: putting your toothbrushes side by side and sharing the same roll of toilet paper, discussing whether or not to change T.V. channels, finding hair in the plughole of the shower cubicle, not being able to sit for a moment in silence without the other person asking "What's wrong?", closing one's eyes peacefully, turning out the light and not feeling afraid, being near. Every night, his father falls asleep first. Around eleven o'clock, his head starts to droop,

75

to nod, he fumbles with the newspaper, as if trying to hold on to one particular page, until finally the night defeats him. His father wears pale striped pyjamas, blue or perhaps grey. He sleeps on his back, with his arms outstretched and his mouth half-open. Andrés is surprised to see this, it almost seems to reveal an excess of trust: his father lies there with such marvellous placidity, certain that nothing will disturb him; he sleeps as if nothing could ever hurt him, as if he were a small boy on a family holiday who has fallen asleep on the grass without a care in the world, knowing that no threat hangs over him. Andrés watches in envy. He, on the other hand, lies on his side, arms folded, almost hunched up, head pressed into the pillow.

His father doesn't snore either. The first night, though, Andrés lay for a long time, listening to his breathing. When they were lying there in the dark, he realised that the quiet sound of his father's breathing was beginning to fill the whole room; he felt that the air was creaking as it entered and left his father's body; he couldn't help recalling a vast catalogue of neoplasms: a section of lung with multiple tumoral nodules like a piece of meat covered in mushrooms, a lymphagitis carcinomatosa in which the lung resembles a dried fish; images of tumoral ulcerations, of parechymal invasions that leave yellowish areas and haemorrhagic foci; images of pulmonary lymphatic territories on the verge of necrosis . . . Unable to sleep, Andrés sat down on the bed and turned on the T.V. again, but continued to watch his father sleeping, on his back, arms outstretched and mouth half-open, resting, as if nothing were happening around him, as if nothing were happening inside his body either. Andrés went over to him, crouched by his bed and again listened to his breathing. He doesn't know how long he stayed there, motionless in the shadows and the oblique light from the T.V. screen, not thinking about anything, quite still, breathing along with his father.

The time when Andrés comes closest to telling his father the truth is the evening they stay on the beach of Puerto Cruz almost until nightfall. They've bought a bottle of red wine and are sitting on the seashore where the waves break on the sand. They drink in silence. But Andrés cannot feel at ease by his father's side; he waits, like a hunter, alert, always ready to leap up and catch the famous ideal moment and thus fulfil the secret reason behind the trip. His father, though, as the days pass, seems to feel more comfortable, calmer, enjoying every moment. They talk a little about everything and, of course, end up, discussing the state of the nation. Everyone does it. It occurs to Andrés that the political situation has probably saved many a married couple who have run out of things to say. At family get-togethers, there's always a ready-made topic of discussion. Politics renews bonds, revives enthusiasms and passions, but it doesn't really work with his father. After a brief exchange of views, they grow bored. Andrés refills their plastic cups with wine.

"Don't you think it's wonderful," he says, as if hoping to create the right atmosphere, "I mean, the two of us being together like this?"

"Yes," says his father slowly, contentedly, looking again at the sea. "Do you know what I find odd?" he adds. "The sea doesn't smell. The sea doesn't smell any more."

Andrés looks at the sea. He breathes in deeply through his nose. His gaze shifts suddenly to the farthest edge of the vast, undulating blue cloth before them. Is this the moment? What can he say? Is this really the place, the ideal moment, to start talking about diagnoses and suggesting a chat about the nosogenesis of a pulmonary condition?

"It doesn't smell of anything," his father says again.

Andrés doesn't dare look at him now, he hears only the faint sigh of a small wave breaking next to them. They're both sitting on the sand, and when the wave washes over them, it only reaches their navels. What is he waiting for? How much longer can he delay mentioning what is becoming increasingly obvious? His father is gazing out to sea, sniffing the air. He's holding his cup of wine in one hand when, all of a sudden, he has a coughing fit, he's doubled up with coughing, the cup trembles in his hand, then falls into the water. He can't stop coughing. Andrés tries to help him, the wine is staining the sea red, the sea has turned to red wine. When his father manages to straighten up, his face is contorted, as if he were suffocating, and then Andrés realises that his father has vomited into the water, has vomited blood, that it isn't wine, the redness surrounding them, dyeing the water around them, spreading the colour towards the horizon, staining the sand red too. The sea is suddenly full of blood, his father's blood.

What does the water smell of now?

Andrés cleans his father up and reassures him. They go to a nearby first-aid post on the road, and then to a pharmacy. Andrés tells him that it's a mild form of food poisoning, that it was probably the tuna in soya oil they ate at lunchtime that has upset his stomach. That night, his father goes to bed early and Andrés takes a sleeping pill. The following day, they have to take the ferry back. He dreams again, and again he can't remember what he dreamt. He wakes up with a dry mouth. As he brushes his teeth, he considers writing a letter, writing his father a long letter, telling him the truth and explaining how difficult it is for him to tell him the truth. He immediately realises what a ridiculous idea this is. Writing a letter is the coward's way out, something you would only do out of fear.

Karina cannot understand how quickly this correspondence has become a compulsion. Since Dr Miranda left for Isla Margarita, Ernesto Durán hasn't stopped writing. Each morning, when she arrives at the office, there's a letter waiting for her. Each evening, before she leaves, Karina sends him a reply that she has slowly, throughout the day, been writing and rewriting, carefully, devotedly drafting and redrafting. She has bought a dictionary so as not to keep repeating the same words. She takes great pains over getting the right tone. That is what she finds hardest. Because sometimes she feels tempted to let herself go and forgets that it's supposed to be Dr Miranda who's writing, even though she knows Dr Miranda would never write quite as she does. There are particular words and turns of phrase that could only come from her. And yet the letters are also half her and half Dr Miranda, a place where their two styles coexist.

Generally speaking, they have kept to strictly clinical matters in their letters. Thus Karina has learned that what Ernesto Durán refers to as *the sickness* – always in italics and virtually omnipresent – started with a case of labyrinthitis or suspected labyrinthitis. One morning, when he got out of bed, he felt as if he had completely lost his sense of balance. In order to remain standing, he had to lean on something or someone. Everything became a walking stick or a banister. After doing the rounds of various specialists, he began a treatment intended to deal with a minor infection of the middle ear. After that, however, every-thing became rather confused. Even though it seemed that the physical problem with his ear had been cured, the symptoms refused to go away. Durán would wake each morning with the same sense of fragile balance. He would stand up and immediately feel that his own body had become a precipice, that at any moment, he might fall. The doctors treating him assured him he was fine, that it was biologically impossible for him to feel what he was feeling or what he said he was feeling; he would insist that he was the only one who knew what was really happening. "Who is the subject of the sickness?" he would ask. "The doctor or the patient?"

Ernesto Durán tried everything, the very latest in Amazonian homeopathy and so-called systemic medicine; he underwent an operation – without surgical instruments and on the banks of a river, near Maracay – performed by a Chinaman who spoke only Portuguese. He also allowed a nun from the convent of San José de Tarbes to place her hands on his abdomen while they said the rosary together. Nothing worked. Only time, Ernesto Durán said, had helped him to live with or, rather, despite his sickness.

The daily presence of the letters, the permanent dialogue with that voice, however, has gradually created a different kind of intimacy. Ernesto Durán has become increasingly important in Karina's life. The other evening, on the metro, she found herself thinking about him. At the weekend, at home, she thought of him again. And she spent a large part of Saturday morning imagining him: Where did he live? What would his apartment be like? Did he make his bed every morning? What did he have in his fridge? Was his place a total mess or was he neurotically tidy? What kind of music did he listen to? Did he have a girlfriend? Was that the real origin of all his ills? Was his divorce the cause of all this suffering?

Karina even dreamed up a scenario in which Ernesto arrived home unexpectedly and found his wife having sex with a neighbour. Right there in the living room. When he opened the door, Ernesto saw his wife naked and licking the penis of the man from apartment 3C. It was one of those dreadful situations, in which no-one knew quite how to react. She withdrew slightly. The neighbour took a step back. Ernesto was trembling. The penis remained erect in the middle of the living room. That was perhaps the worst, the most brutal thing: that his neighbour's penis should show no respect and remain quite unaffected by the situation. She wiped her lips with her hand. Ernesto stared at her, astonished, paralysed by surprise. The neighbour appeared to have eyes only for his clothes in a pile on the floor, as if he were lost at sea and searching desperately around for a rubber ring or a lifebelt. When she realised what she was doing, Karina instinctively shook her head, trying to drive that threesome out of her Saturday morning. That was when she first began to feel anxious: why was she thinking about such things? What were they doing inside her head, Ernesto Durán's ex-wife and the neighbour? What the hell did all that have to do with her?

"You're getting hooked," says Adelaida in a mischievous, singsong voice.

Adelaida is her copy editor. Every afternoon, she reads the latest missive, offers opinions and criticisms, and suggests changes, always erring on the side of boldness. She suffers none of the doubts or pangs of conscience that sometimes trouble Karina. Adelaida is determined to see in this story the seeds of a Hollywood romance. If Karina had a partner or a boyfriend, or at least slept with someone once a week, she probably wouldn't have been so easily captivated, trapped like an insect, by the words of that imaginary invalid, that madman. So, at least, Adelaida thinks. Perhaps it's fate. The roads of loneliness are infinite, she says.

Karina is confused too. The imminent return of Dr Miranda makes her even more nervous. She doesn't think it's possible to keep up this farce for very much longer. Sooner or later, Ernesto Durán will phone or come looking for Andrés Miranda. And what then? What will happen then? Inevitably, in less than a second, the very thing that had seemed to her harmless and amusing will become dangerous and tragic. She's filled with anxiety. She can't understand how she could have gone so far, she can't understand how she could have allowed herself to be persuaded to answer that letter, passing herself off as the doctor. She should never have taken that first fatal step. Lying is a hard drug to kick, and now she doesn't know how to extricate herself from that lie, how to get rid of it. She isn't even sure she wants to. Each time she writes, Karina feels as if she were standing on an invisible line, on a knife-edge separating two very different types of words: on the one hand, there are the dry, sober, business-like, opaque, correct, well-chosen but dull words; on the other, are the brilliant, sharp, lush, disorderly, carnivorous, voluptuous, uncontrollable words. She's finding it harder and harder to keep the balance. She's gradually losing confidence in herself.

The day before Dr Miranda comes back to work, the usual morning letter turns suddenly into a real emergency:

Dear Andrés,
I've been up all night vomiting and with a high fever. The nausea won't go away and my blood pressure's very high. I can't even get out of bed.
My phone number is 551 4978. As soon as you read this, please call me.
Your friend,
Ernesto

The journey back seems longer. It's almost as if the afternoon light were stopping the ferry from travelling any faster. The mood among the passengers is different too. They're all going home, the sand is slowly trickling from their memories; everyone on deck seems filled by a slight sense of disillusionment. Andrés, moreover, feels frustrated and disappointed with himself. He has lied to Mariana on the phone; he didn't have the courage to tell her that he hadn't been able to do what he'd intended to do on this trip. That lie makes him feel even more vulnerable. It's a multiplication of his own stupidity. That very morning, in Pampatar, on his father's insistence, he had again behaved absurdly. He had to find a way to complete the lie that had been the whole justification for the holiday. Ever since they arrived, his father had kept reminding him that they had come to the island to see a house which someone was supposedly offering him as part-payment of a debt. It had been a rather tangled and ambiguous story, never fleshed out with too many details, but on the island, where it had to become fact, the story proved almost too fragile to survive.

"Aren't we going to see that house, then?" his father asked, somewhat puzzled, over their breakfast of fresh fruit.

"Yes, of course, that's what we're going to do this morning."

By the side of the road, on the way to Pampatar, Andrés spotted a condominium under construction. He didn't know what else to do. He braked rather sharply, hurriedly explained to his father that this was the housing complex they had come to see, but then insisted that he stay in the car.

"Wait for me here," he said, before striding off towards the building site.

He spoke to an engineer and with some workmen who, in

83

rather desultory fashion, were putting the finishing touches to the roof of one of the houses. He asked ridiculous questions and waved his arms about, so that his father, from a distance, would assume that he was talking business, asking about practical details to do with the architecture of the houses, that he was finally dealing with the real reason for their trip. He managed somehow to stretch this out for fifteen minutes. The engineer began to think Andrés must be mad, either that or an idiot determined to waste his time. Then, most absurd of all, as he took his leave, Andrés embraced him. The engineer then thought that he was not only an idiot, but a poofter too. Andrés went back to the car to tell his father a new pack of lies. His father didn't like the houses.

"I don't think it's a good deal," he said.

Andrés remembers the scene and feels faintly amused, but somehow pathetic too. It's all part of the same overarching emotion. Perhaps it simply angers him to see himself being so weak, so incapable of dealing with the situation. He's done it so often, with so many people, even cruelly, without a scrap of pity, feeling that he was doing the right thing, that frankness should, ethically speaking, be part of the medical armoury. Now, however, he finds himself caught up in a whole circus of infinite procrastinations. His father comes over to him, carrying two coffees. One with milk, one black.

"Are you alright?" he asks.

The lights of La Guaira are getting ever closer. Andrés looks at him and knows he has no choice now.

"What's wrong?" asks his father, realising from his son's anxious face that something is up.

Andrés puts his hands together and clears his throat. The words feel almost like heartburn inside him. He can feel the

vowels scraping against his oesophagus, the consonants rush-
ing towards the roof of his mouth. It's inevitable. He can do
nothing to stop it now. That's how it is sometimes. You always
end up speaking when you hadn't intended to, when you
weren't expecting to, when there are no more "better moments".
Sometimes the words just say themselves, speak for themselves.

"You've got cancer, Dad," Andrés blurts out, albeit quietly.
There are some things that can only be said quietly.

II

He wishes it were all much hazier, he wishes his memory of that afternoon were not so very clear, that it had receded a little, that, with the passing of time, it, too, had gradually faded and sunk into the whole pointless compendium of the past. But no, that afternoon is still there, sharp, wounding, rough; ever since then, behind every afternoon, there is always that other afternoon, so much more solid and so resistant to being forgotten. Andrés has done everything possible to make it disappear, but it's no use. It's a stain that nothing can wash out, that never goes. For two whole weeks, Andrés has kept seeing himself in that afternoon, every afternoon, always that same afternoon, one afternoon inside another, repeating over and over:

"You've got cancer, Dad."

His father was completely taken aback. Andrés couldn't meet his gaze and turned away, ashamed. In the background was the port of La Guaira, intermittently illuminated. They stood for a few seconds in silence, then his father said:

"Look at me."

Andrés wouldn't, but his father insisted:

"Look at me."

He didn't need to raise his voice. His tone was strong and authoritative.

"Look at me, damn it!"

When Andrés did finally turn to face him, he saw a shaken, tearful man. It would be hard to say exactly what emotion was troubling him most just then: surprise? fear? indignation? rage?

His chin was trembling. His father's face suddenly turned incredibly pale, like a sudden white blush. Andrés could almost hear the teeth crunching inside that tight, tremulous jaw. His father dropped his coffee cup, and when it hit the floor, the plastic cracked and the hot liquid splattered Andrés' shoes.

"How long have you known?"

Andrés again felt like a child hauled up in front of his father, he thought again that the whole trip had been a terrible, stupid mistake. His father spoke to him again as his father. For a moment, they ceased being two adults, who were occasionally friends and occasionally not, who shared a common history; for a moment, they returned to that age when they really could only be father and son, nothing more.

"Does that matter?"

"It does to me."

Andrés shifted uneasily on his feet, made an attempt at a gesture, opened his mouth to speak, then said nothing.

"You knew right from the start, didn't you? From the first tests."

Andrés could find no sounds to make. He felt as if words had suddenly deserted him.

"I asked you not to lie to me, Andrés. That was all I asked of you."

"I didn't lie to you," Andrés said in a whisper.

"No, of course not. You just concealed the truth from me!"

"If you'll let me explain . . ."

"So that was what this trip was all about." His father spoke with bitter sarcasm, then, with scorn. "To give me the big news!"

Then he turned abruptly and went over to a rail almost at the front of the boat. Andrés hesitated for a moment. He sensed that his father was crying or trying very hard not to. He waited

88

a few minutes before joining him. He imagined that would be best, that his father needed time to quell his anger, his rage. Then, very slowly, he walked over to him, trying to be as discreet as possible. His father did not turn round, but kept his back to him. The port was getting nearer.

"You didn't dare," he muttered hoarsely.

"No."

"You had thousands of opportunities. We were together on beaches, we slept in the same room . . ."

"I couldn't do it. Whenever I tried to tell you, I just couldn't."

"But you could now," added his father somewhat resentfully.

"Yes, I don't know what came over me. But that certainly wasn't how I wanted to tell you. I'm sorry."

Very slowly, his father turned round. Andrés could see that his eyes were wet with tears and that beneath those tears lay something resembling both melancholy and rancour, some emotion for which the dictionary did not yet have a word.

"I'm sorry," Andrés murmured again, as if he could go on repeating those words for the rest of the journey. As if those were the only words he had to hand, the only ones left to him. Still keeping his distance, his father said:

"All this makes me think that it's not something straightforward." He looked at him with eyebrows raised interrogatively. "If it was nothing very serious, you wouldn't have found it so hard, we wouldn't have come on this trip."

"Yes, it's serious," mumbled Andrés awkwardly.

"Say that again."

This was an order.

"Say that again. Tell me that it's 'serious'. Tell me the whole truth now."

They both fell silent, looking at each other. How long did

they stand like that? His memory doesn't tell him. That is one thing he can't remember. He only has that frozen image of them, studying each other, saying nothing. Until an acid teardrop cuts the image in two, from top to bottom, like a knife, tearing the scene apart. Andrés could no longer hold back his tears. However hard he blinked, he couldn't do it: that was his response. Like a confused and cornered child, forced to accept that there's no way out. He could barely manage a mumbled "Forgive me, Dad," his voice broken by sobs.

Javier Miranda stared at him, astonished, overwhelmed. He appeared to be trembling or trying hard to keep his body from trembling. He bowed his head, turned and walked off into the shadows.

They got into the car in silence, left the port and drove up the motorway to Caracas still in silence. On two or three occasions, Andrés tried to start a conversation, but received no response. His father remained mute throughout the journey, staring straight ahead. Andrés imagined that the news had left him paralysed, that he was still taking in that information, as invasive as a scalpel. When they stopped outside his father's apartment building, Andrés got out to help him take his suitcase from the boot. Then he made to accompany him to the door, carrying the suitcase, but his father stopped him.

"Thanks, I can do it," he said in an oddly gentle tone.

Still wrapped in that same silence, he set off towards the door. Andrés watched him, every nerve tensed. When he could stand it no longer, he shouted:

"Would you have preferred not to know?"

His father stopped, but didn't turn to look at him.

Andrés asked again: "Would it have been better if I hadn't told you?"

His father stood for a moment as if pondering the question, as if the question were a peach stone under his tongue. Then, sadly, he went up to the door and into the building. Without saying a word. Without turning round.

Why should this happen to me? Why me? Ever since that night, Javier Miranda keeps asking these questions over and over. As if it were a personal matter, as if he were addressing nature's complaints department and had sat down to talk to the manager. Why me? Why should this happen to me? – while he submits to more tests, more examinations. Why me? Why should this happen to me? – when the oncologist speaks to him in incomprehensible jargon. Why me? Why should this happen to me? – as he starts a new session of chemotherapy.

"How are you feeling today?" asks the nurse with a smile.

"I'd rather have been run over by a car."

Ever since that night, everything has changed. First, there's his state of mind. He can't shake off the depression that doesn't so much wrap around him as drench him. He's angry with life, furious, resentful; he feels powerless, terrified, knowing that there's no escape. Finally, and in the very worst possible way, when he's almost seventy, he has learned the cruel meaning of the word "fate". This is it. That's all. A syringe. His relationship with his son has changed too. In fact, his relationship with everyone has changed: and that, of course, includes Andrés. He no longer knows how to treat him, what to do, what to say to him. Deep down, he feels sorry for the others, he regrets what's happening, he'd like to spare everyone else this whole pointless process, this exhausting task. When he sees them, he invariably bows his head. He knows how awkward the situation is for them as well. Perhaps it would all be easier if he tried to look happy, if he pretended, if he behaved as if nothing were happening. Perhaps that would be ideal for everyone, to die discreetly, without anyone noticing, without anyone realising.

The most marked change, however, is in his body. Javier Miranda feels that he has lost it, that it no longer belongs to him. He has never felt that before, never felt so clearly the stark divide caused by illness. Now he's dramatically aware of a separation between him and his own body. He is apart, inhabiting a damaged structure, inside a skin he no longer governs, that no longer speaks to him, that has another government now, that does not answer him, that lives for itself and for its own destruction.

Sometimes, at night, before sleeping, he feels this with exasperating clarity. He's in the bathroom, standing at the mirror, holding his toothbrush, looking at himself. It's the last ritual of the day. He hasn't even turned on the light. Only the lamp in the corridor dimly illuminates his image in the glass. He sees it then – so painfully clearly! He can feel its presence in everything – in his hair, in the shine in his eyes, in the colour of his skin, even in the shape of his head. The illness is doing something he hadn't thought possible: it's taking over his very physiognomy. In the early hours, one Wednesday, after peeing, as he passed the bathroom mirror, he noticed, out of the corner of his eye, the bones beneath the skin, the ever more evident shape of his skull. As if the mirror were an X-ray.

"Who's coming to fetch you today?" asks the nurse, helping his body to sit down in a chair in the corridor.

"My daughter-in-law," whispers Javier Miranda.

"Well, I'll leave you here then," says the woman. "Now you just sit and wait for her, alright?"

He merely nods sadly, his lips sagging, hanging down

towards his jaw. The doctors and the nurses know as well. They don't talk to him, they converse with his body, with that other creature who has to be treated like an idiot child, with that wound that can barely stand, that will soon collapse completely.

While he waits, a nun walks past him along the corridor. She's accompanying an old lady who is clearly in the final stages. Perhaps that's how he looks too. The woman is walking very cautiously, looking fearfully around her. Perhaps she simply wants to escape from this torment, this aseptic horror. The nun by her side is wearing a long, floor-length habit, so that you can't see her feet. When she walks, she seems to be floating. She's a nun floating down a hospital corridor. She's wearing a wooden cross around her neck. Jesus Christ experienced death, he thinks suddenly, but he never experienced illness. The gods die, they don't fall ill. That's their advantage.

As soon as he started studying medicine, Andrés Miranda knew that his vocation was not entirely pure. In a way, he always felt incomplete because he didn't share the other students' surgical passion; he was more interested in slides and microscopes than in the practical sessions; he preferred the blackboard to the scalpel. While his colleagues couldn't wait to get down to some practical work, Andrés was happy to postpone that moment. The idea of being in an operating theatre, dealing with some emergency, didn't excite him at all. It didn't repel him either, but it obviously wasn't the clinical area for which he felt most enthusiasm. He always felt it was a purely personal thing, and felt more drawn to research, to observation and analysis, than to the practical application of medicine. Many years later, reading *The Wounded Body*, an invaluable philosophical dictionary written by Cristóbal Pera, Andrés at last found the words he had so needed to read during his first years at university: "If we use the *war-like language* so often used as a global metaphor in surgery, the *cruel* surgical operation is an *act of violence*, in which physical force is needed to penetrate the patient's anatomical space, to subjugate the 'enemy' – the sickness made concrete in the lesion – to disarm and destroy it." That definition perfectly described a spirit, an inner attitude that Andrés did not have, had never had. The thought of actually *invading* another body didn't thrill him in the least. Even assuming that it was necessary and was an *act of salvation*, his medical vocation seemed always to be somewhere else, stirred by different impulses. Cristóbal Pera adds: "Surgical *violence* has created the image of the surgeon's *power* over the patient and the latter's surrender in a ritual of submission." Nevertheless, for Andrés, the power lay elsewhere, in the space occupied by knowledge. This was his way of coming to terms with what might be considered a weakness. He preferred the knowledge of books to the knowledge of the hands.

He still remembers how the time he spent working in hospitals was always the most tiresome part of the whole course. Understanding how bodies work was still his passion, but doing something to a living body, interfering in another's breathing, intervening in another's blood, invading another's flesh, was not an important part of his vocation. He never rejected the experience, but he probably never enjoyed it either. The idea of knowing that he was before, on or in a living body slightly inhibited his own motivation, his own skill. It wasn't the bodies that intimidated him, but knowing that he had a definite responsibility towards them. Perhaps that's why he felt more comfortable with corpses.

In his university days, corpses were divided into two groups:

the mummies and the freshers. The names said everything. The stiffs, which had been used before, belonged to the first group; the newly dead to the second category. No-one liked working with the mummies. It was like being with a dummy, it always felt slightly unreal. The mummy was like an old vinyl record that has become more and more chipped over time. A mummy might have a couple of toes missing from its right foot. Once, some joker stubbed out a cigarette on the cheek of a dead boy. That kind of thing happened with the mummies. Any sessions with them gave rise to laughter, childish jokes, distance. The freshers, on the other hand, provoked, at least initially, silence and a strange intimacy.

For Andrés, corpses were an ideal middle path, halfway between books and the emergency operation. They weren't the mere illustration of a text; they had volume, presence, they were real bodies and yet, at the same time, not entirely real, not the whole truth: they lacked warmth, feeling, urgency. It was precisely in that unreal reality that Andrés found his place. So much so that, more than once, he had wondered if his destiny didn't lie in performing autopsies; he felt almost condemned to the field of diagnosing lifeless bodies, in which the only signs are the past, in which nothing beats and everything is merely mark or trace. For a long time, he felt his vocation was closer to producing "damage reports" than to "the saving of lives". He belonged to the group or league who always arrive when there's nothing to be done, when all that's needed is a signature on the final balance sheet.

As he progressed in his career, it became clearer to him that in his professional life he was more suited to research or teaching. The prospect of dealing with patients on a daily basis, as part of his work routine, became less and less attractive. It implied a risk he wasn't sure he wanted to run – making a mistake. Making a mistake in a laboratory was quite different from doing so in an operating theatre. At the time, Andrés began to fall under the spell of the famous Flemish doctor, Andreas Vesalius. He shared with him not only a first name, but a passion for study, a fascination with how the human body works. From him he also learned that curiosity is a high-risk occupation and that peering in at the enigmas of medicine can prove fatal.

Andreas Vesalius was born in Brussels in 1514. He was a brilliant man and considered to be the founder of modern anatomy. He studied in Paris, taught at Leuven, became a professor at Bologna University, and ended up working as a doctor in the imperial court of Charles V. In 1543, he published his work *De humani corporis fabrica libri septem*, a ground-breaking study of the structure of the human body that openly questioned Galen's theories. The book was illustrated with more than three hundred engravings that showed human anatomy as it had never been shown before in the history of civilisation. From early on, Vesalius had made his mark on history. He would probably have gone on to do much more, but his life was touched by tragedy: in 1561, in Madrid, the court of the Holy Inquisition sentenced him to death.

Vesalius honed his talents largely on the work he did on dissecting corpses. He had also been given the necessary permissions and blessings to carry out this work. As far as one can ascertain, one fateful day, a body betrayed science: Vesalius opened up a dead man who wasn't dead. Beneath the skin, beneath the thorax, a heart was still beating. Very feebly perhaps. Perhaps the last flicker of a life about to be extinguished. There was nothing to be done. But in that moment, science became a sin. Some studies say that the body belonged to a nobleman close to the throne, which seems unlikely, but what is known is that Philip II spoke up for Vesalius before the Inquisition and saved his life. One legend has it that the doctor was dressed in sackcloth and sandals and, to pay for his error, was condemned to wander the desert for the rest of his life. Another version of the story has the same tragic tone: Andreas Vesalius paid for his guilt by making a long pilgrimage to the Holy Land. On the way back from Jerusalem, the ship in which he was travelling was wrecked in strange circumstances, taking Vesalius down with it. Thus he paid for his curiosity: either devoured by the desert or by the sea. Drowned in the void.

"Don't succumb to Vesalius Syndrome," Professor Armando Coll often said to them. "Don't let that paralyse you."

One afternoon, after class, he went for a drink with his students in a small, insalubrious restaurant called La Estrella China. It was near the university and the students went there because the booze was cheap enough for them to get drunk without spending the whole of their allowance. Professor Coll ordered a whisky. After two hours, and feeling less sober and in a more confiding mood, he confessed that he himself was a hostage to Vesalius Syndrome. That's what he called it. He found the story terrifying. He couldn't understand how humanity could have punished one of its most outstanding geniuses like that. "Vesalius was almost another Da Vinci," he said. Andrés Miranda drank in every word, full of surprise and admiration. Before taking his leave, Professor Coll looked at them with a kind of melancholy pity.

"All it proves," he said, "is that the birth of medicine is irremediably bound up with the birth of negligence. They are two inseparable practices, living side by side. Prepare yourselves."

*

At first, she counted them one by one: she got as far as nine. She could stand it no longer. Ever since the morning of that brief and terrible letter in which Ernesto Durán begged for help, nine days had passed and she had done nothing. There was nothing she could do. She couldn't phone Durán, nor could she tell Dr Miranda what had happened. She'd been left locked up alone with her anxiety. Then more days passed; she didn't count them this time, but there were a lot. Too many. Ernesto Durán never wrote again. Nor did he phone. Each morning, though, she repeated the same ritual and rather longingly looked for a letter from him in Dr Miranda's in-box. Nothing. The last she'd heard from him was that brief message, that cry for help, giving his phone number. Sometimes she's assailed by the image of that e-mail and then she can see Ernesto Durán lying on his bed, very pale, mouth half-open, his breathing laboured. He hasn't shaved for days. He looks feebly upwards, as if his eyes barely had the strength to see as far as the ceiling. The bed is filthy. There are pools of vomit. The image is filled with the stench of shit and urine. She's also imagined him lying on the floor of his apartment, as if he'd managed to drag himself a few yards before fainting. He's naked. He's been dead for two days. His skin is turning dark, almost violet in colour. His mouth is open. An insect buzzes and dances, like a tiny vulture, over the awful stillness of his corpse.

Ernesto has slipped into her nights as well. At two in the morning, Karina starts fearfully awake: in her dream world, Ernesto Durán is holding a knife with which he's cutting his femoral artery. The blood spurts out and spatters the whole dream.

"If you're that worried, why don't you call him?" Adelaida

says, appealing to her common sense and meanwhile chewing on a raw carrot. They're both on a diet again.

"What would I say to him?"

"Don't say anything. At least you'll know he's well, that he's alive. Do you want me to phone him?"

Karina shakes her head. When she saw that he was no longer sending e-mails, she had tried phoning him herself on various occasions and at various times. She just wanted to hear his voice and then hang up, nothing more. She just needed to be sure he was safe. But no-one ever answered. The phone just rang and rang.

She has also considered going to see him. She found his address in his medical file. He lives in the centre, near Avenida Fuerzas Armadas, on the corner of San Ramón. She could always leave work a little early one evening and simply go over there. She could, for example, wait on the pavement across from his building for a while, where she wouldn't look too obvious, just to see if he went in or out, to make sure he was still alive.

"Do you feel guilty?" Adelaida unleashes the question without warning, one evening when they're both leaning at the bar of Las Cibeles. "Because that's what it looks like."

"No, I just can't stand not knowing what happened, not hearing from him. That's all. Does that seem odd to you? He sends that message and then . . . nothing. Absolute silence, he's just vanished."

"Perhaps he's punishing you."

"Me? If he's punishing anyone, it's Dr Miranda."

"Perhaps he got fed up and realised that the doctor's never going to help him, that it's all a bit of leg-pull, that he's never going to take him seriously. Perhaps that was the final test. And now it's over. The guy disappears for ever."

But Karina's anxieties are not so easily soothed. That same evening, she stays late after work and decides to try one last thing. She feels more desperation than fear, which is why she takes the risk of writing another letter.

Dear Ernesto,

First of all, I must apologise for taking so long to reply to your last e-mail. Unfortunately, as I warned you, I had some urgent business to attend to away from Caracas. For reasons beyond my control, I then had to go on somewhere else and couldn't check my e-mail for several days. And that's why I couldn't answer your call for help.

When I did finally get to my e-mail, it was too late. I've been calling the number you sent me, but no-one ever answers. I apologise again for this situation and I quite understand if you're upset and, given that it was an emergency, I do hope you sought help from someone else. But please let me know that you're alright and were able to cope satisfactorily with the situation.

Hoping to hear from you soon,

Andrés

Ever since the illness installed itself between them, their relationship has become less fluid, pricklier, more difficult. Now there are three of them. There is always an invisible weight between them. They are father and son plus one, the other, a third unnameable force that never leaves them alone. They spend a lot more time together, but time is different now. They talk less and less. They know it, they feel it, but they don't know how to express it, what to do. It may be that both of them would like to leave, run away, never see each other again, but they daren't do that either. They can't bear the thought that they will say goodbye like this, although they have no option. In more than one sense – although it's a dreadful cliché – there is no easy remedy.

Andrés goes with him to the chemotherapy sessions and tries to be with him in the apartment after four in the afternoon, when Merny has left. She has finally agreed to come every day to his father's apartment, although it sometimes seems that she doesn't want to get too involved. Andrés thinks she's just protecting herself, that she doesn't want to share in his father's death. Perhaps that's partly how they all feel: the certain sense of imminent death produces other forms of life.

The kids are aware that something's going on too. They may not know precisely what it is, but they know. It's not just their grandfather's pallor, the hair loss and the look of resigned sadness that seems to have settled in his eyes. Behind the grown-ups' pact of silence, there's something that not even his clinical appearance can conceal. It's hard to define, barely palpable, but, at the same time, obvious. It's there. It's a managed, domesticated violence, but by no means submissive or tame. It remains a brutal violence. Right before their eyes, a life is being pitilessly laid waste, swept away. There's a lot of gauze, a lot of cleanliness, a lot of qualified staff, but there's no pity. It's a crime to which there are far too many witnesses, a legalised crime, a crime no-one can stop.

In Christa Wolf's novel, *In the Flesh*, a woman in hospital realises with horror: "There's someone trying to murder me." Exactly. *She* is. Her own illness is. Andrés shouldn't read books like this, but he seeks them out, with ever more determination; perhaps he's trying to find in their pages what he can't resolve at the hospital, at home, at the cinema, or over family lunches on Sundays. Some nights, he reads into the small hours. He's closed his office for a month.

"I'm on holiday," he said.

And yet that isn't enough. Whenever he's alone with his father, he doesn't know what to say, how to look at him. Javier Miranda seems to feel the same. He doesn't say anything either. He stares at the floor or mutters some brief response, says he's tired and falls asleep or pretends to. Andrés stays with him, in silence. It seems to him cruel, absurd. This is exactly what will await them both when it finally happens. Silence. This is their sole destiny. Silence. This is precisely what they both fear and what hurts them most. Silence.

Perhaps he's imagining his death. Perhaps his father is thinking about that all the time, about the exact situation, the precise moment when his existence will end. When Andrés thinks about his own death, he has more fears than certainties. A recurring image troubles him: he's with some friends at a restaurant. Everyone is eating, drinking and talking. Suddenly, he suffers a massive heart attack. Out of the blue. No burning sensation in the stomach, no shooting pains up the left arm. It's like a gunshot, like a bullet that doesn't leave his body, but stays inside, that fells him in half a second. That's the last thing Andrés sees: a few glasses, an ashtray, an almost empty bread basket . . . that is his final landscape as he crashes face-down on the table.

But his father would never have imagined that his death would be the way it presents itself to him now. Sickness is a mistake, a bureaucratic blunder on nature's part, an absolute lack of efficiency. Everyone wants a swift death that lasts only a second, that is as surprising as it is lethal. It's a very deep desire, part of the human condition. Sudden death is almost a utopia.

His father, however, avoids thinking. He resists, he forces his imagination or his memories to move on whenever he feels those thoughts approaching, trying to corral him. At first, immediately after they got back from Isla Margarita, he started doing inexplicable things. Every morning, he would walk to the newspaper kiosk three blocks from his house, buy a pack of cigarettes and, on the way back, break each cigarette in half, one by one. He kept up this routine for a week and a half, every morning.

Then he started buying things he didn't need. One Saturday, he went to the Chinese market and bought various bottled sauces, bean sprouts and other herbs that he subsequently threw in the bin. One afternoon, he went to the building where he had worked for thirty-eight years. He stood at the door, as if stunned, just looking. He saw himself going in through that door, every day, for years and years. He saw himself in different suits, the pale grey one, the brown one he bought in December, the blue one with the wide lapels, and the different ties he wore. It was a film repeating the same shot ad infinitum, that one brief scene. For thirty-eight years, Javier Miranda worked as an administrator for the oil industry. First, when they were still American-owned companies, and after they were nationalised too, but always in the same building. At sixty-five they retired him, him and his whole generation. He doesn't know for how long he stood there. He thought about going in, about going up to the eighth floor, but felt afraid. He probably wouldn't know anyone now, and no-one would know who he was. He walked home. He was walking for several hours.

His habits changed too. He stopped watching television. He even lost interest in baseball. But sometimes, he would spend hours in silence, staring at the blank screen, watching the faint reflection of his body in the lifeless, opaque glass. Even at moments like that, he didn't want to think, he wanted just to sit there in the void and let drowsiness and lethargy sweep over him. But that's not possible. Sooner or later, he has to stop running away, the attempted escape always fails. How would you like to die? Now he thinks that we should all have the right to answer that question.

This evening, while his father is sleeping, the phone suddenly rings. Andrés answers, but the person calling immediately hangs up. When this happens again with exactly the same result, Andrés concludes that this cannot be mere chance. The person ringing doesn't want to speak to him. He becomes suspicious. His father doesn't have a service that identifies the caller, and so he can't even find out where the call came from. Who could it have been? Someone who doesn't want to speak to him. Why?

A week later, the same thing happens. His father is having a shower. He's getting steadily weaker, but he still resists being helped by Andrés. It also embarrasses him for his son to see him naked, "like a wet chicken". The phone rings. Andrés answers, says Hello, and immediately the other person hangs up. It happens again. Now, though, Andrés picks up the phone and says nothing. He can almost feel the breathing at the other end, a hesitation wrapped in a breath. It's only a matter of seconds, but he can touch them, feel them. Then suddenly:

"Is that you?"

Surprise paralyses him. The woman's voice disarms him, he doesn't know what to say. She immediately ends the call. He hears the click of the phone being put down.

"Who was it?" asks his father from the bathroom.

Andrés hesitates before replying. Then, as if testing him out, he says:

"I don't know. They hung up when they heard my voice."

"Perhaps it was a wrong number," says his father softly, after a pause, and without much conviction.

Andrés makes of this possibly unimportant detail an enigma that he tries obsessively to resolve. Mariana even pokes gentle fun at him for this. Perhaps it's mere coincidence, a banal fact of his father's day-to-day life. But nothing is the same for Andrés any more. Or so it seems. He suddenly feels that he has never paid much attention to his father's private life. He has never known him to have a girlfriend or partner or even a fleeting affair. Nor was he ever very interested. But now, that woman's voice on the phone has become a source of curiosity: it uncovers all kinds of questions that Andrés has never asked himself, a slice of his father's life of which he knows nothing. It's true that Javier Miranda never remarried. He devoted himself entirely to bringing up his son and then, when Andrés got married, he carried on working and cultivated a routine that seemed to have no room for love or sex.

"Your dad has a right to a private life too, you know," Mariana says. "Perhaps he did have girlfriends, but didn't want you to find out. There's no reason why you should know everything."

But Andrés wants to know everything. He leaves his father with Merny at the hospital for another session of chemo, and goes straight back to the apartment. He wants to poke around, rummage, pry, as if he were a private detective. Javier Miranda's bedroom is fairly austere. No decorative details. A double bed with blue sheets, two pillows, a wooden bedside table on which there is a lamp, a book and a remote control for the T.V. The book is one Andrés gave him a few weeks ago. The jokey, slightly nostalgic memoirs of a Caracas journalist. It was the only thing Andrés and Mariana thought he might like.

Grey curtains at the windows. A large wardrobe, with two wide doors. Andrés opens them gently, as if not wanting to make any noise. There's a shelf on which sit three photos: one of Andrés' mother, one of Andrés and his father crouched together on a beach; the third of Andrés, Mariana and the grandchildren. The clothes hang there, still and perfect. Andrés opens the drawers and glances inside. At that moment, he feels ashamed, embarrassed. It strikes him as rather ridiculous being there, behind his father's back, handling things, looking through his father's underwear, riffling through his shirts. What is he looking for? What does he really want to find? Is it possible to find a life that's over, that might already be lost to them both?

In the drawer of the bedside table he comes across an envelope stuffed with letters. Again he feels ashamed, dishonest, but he has come too far now, there's no point in turning back. They are short letters, unsigned, but clearly in a woman's hand-writing. Or so Andrés believes. Besides, the letters themselves tell him this. They appear to be brief declarations of love, either delivered by hand to his letter box or slipped under the door. No dates, no names, no concrete details. It all seems to indicate a clandestine affair, one that must be kept hidden. One note in particular attracts his attention: it's written on the back of half a dry-cleaning ticket. Just two lines: "I dropped by this afternoon. I wanted to surprise you. I needed a kiss. I needed you."

There's a book in the drawer too: *Dying with Dignity* by Hans Küng and Walter Jens. Andrés can't help feeling a slight tremor. Where would his father have got that book? The top right-hand corner of page 35 is turned down. That's as far as he must have got. Perhaps he stopped on that very page last night. Andrés reads the chapter heading: *Euthanasia discussed: the merciful death*. He closes the book and the drawer. The fact that his father has it hidden away in there means that he doesn't want anyone else to see it. And anyone else means Andrés.

His father and Merny have made a pact. Or, rather, he has imposed a pact on her. They both reached crisis point one afternoon, when they were alone together in the apartment. He was having a really bad reaction to the chemotherapy. The immediate after-effects were ghastly: he felt dreadful, his blood pressure was low, he was feeling dizzy and nauseous, and he was taking epamin to avoid possible convulsions. He'd had a chemo session earlier that morning. At lunchtime, Merny had served him what the nutritionist had recommended. He ate reluctantly, muttering and protesting.

"It all tastes the same," he said.

Merny did not respond. She wasn't having a good day either. Willmer had been out all night. She hadn't been able to sleep. He'd been behaving oddly for some time, and she knew something was wrong. The neighbours said her son was getting into bad company, that he'd been seen with boys from another barrio.

"Not good," thought Merny.

Not good meant crack, guns, police, prison and cemeteries. Willmer finally got in at six in the morning. Merny wanted to slap him, but didn't dare. Jofre didn't either. After all, he wasn't the boy's father. Willmer went straight to his room, without saying a word, he appeared to be under the influence of drugs. Merny left for work, because she has to work, because she can't miss a day, because now more than ever she needs money to get Willmer out of the barrio. That's the only solution. Send him somewhere far away from there. To her sister in the country, for example. That, she thinks, is the only way to save him.

The old man leapt out of bed and ran screaming to the bathroom. He just had time to kneel down by the toilet bowl, but it was too late, he had already vomited his guts up on the way there. The corridor and the bathroom floor were a real mess. In the washbasin, too, there were the remains of his lunch mixed up with other fluids, saliva and dribble, remnants of Javier Miranda's own body. He stayed hunched over the toilet bowl, trying to withstand the retching. He let out a low roar. Everything the body expels stinks, is disgusting and shameful, repellent leftovers no-one wants to see, that should be swiftly cleaned up, covered up, erased. That's what Merny's there for.

But Merny had her own crisis. She vomited up her existence in another way. She exploded. She screamed. She'd had enough. She took off her apron and flung it down. She couldn't help it. There she was, just about to leave, having left everything spotless. She had her own dirt, in her own house, far away, in another world. She didn't want any more work to do. For a moment, the scene seemed utterly incomprehensible. The old man hugging the toilet bowl, coughing and groaning, and Merny standing nearby, beating the wall with her fist, shouting and crying. They remained like that for a while, two bodies furiously flailing and protesting, until gradually they calmed down, not looking at each other, not touching, each in their own place, letting their breathing return to normal.

Between them, they cleaned it all up. They had to put bleach on the floor and the tiles. The fetid smell had invaded the apartment. It was like a second skin tattooed on every object. The apartment was like the belly of some infected animal. Javier invited her to go out somewhere for a drink. Merny declined, embarrassed, saying she really should go straight home. In the end, he made her go with him. They went to a nearby café. She didn't want to order anything, so he ordered them each a coffee. When they finally felt able to talk, the first thing Merny did was to apologise. The old man had a hard time convincing her that it wasn't necessary. It was even harder to get her to open up and tell him what was going on in her life. That was when they made their pact. Javier Miranda offered to give her all the money she needed to send Willmer off to Los Andes, where one of Merny's sisters lived. In exchange, they would have a private agreement, behind Andrés' back.

"No more special diets, alright? No more of that disgusting grilled chicken with no salt. I want olive oil, I want butter, I want sweet things."

"But Dr Andrés says that . . ."

"It doesn't matter what my son says. Merny, look at me. Do you really think I don't know I'm going to die?"

"We're all going to die, Señor Javier," she said, lowering her voice and looking away.

"Yes, we're all going to die. But I'm going first. I'm dying already."

The name of the dry-cleaner's is De Luxe. This was all Andrés could make out on the half ticket he found in his father's bedroom. Then it was simply a matter of calling directory enquiries, getting the telephone number, phoning and asking for their address. Now he's standing outside the shop. He's spent days pondering that woman's voice. On at least two occasions, he's tried to have a conversation with his father about love and marriage. Once, he even attempted to probe deeper into his private life.

"I can understand you not marrying again, but have you never even had an affair?"

"I've never been one for affairs," his father replied vaguely.

"Didn't you even occasionally go with a prostitute? What did you do with your sex life all those years?"

This line of questioning got him nowhere. Javier Miranda merely smiled faintly, almost ingenuously, a mere gesture, barely completed, and said nothing more. As the days passed, the voice of that woman on the phone kept gnawing away at Andrés. He began to hear it more and more often, to stumble over the sound of it again and again. It was the only clue he had. That voice. And a dry-cleaner's.

He'd done his research almost innocently, without giving it much importance, but now that he's actually outside the shop, he can't help feeling a certain unease again. He's thought it all through, but is unsure quite how to proceed. There's a number written in red ink on the left-hand corner of the ticket, presumably the customer reference number. That should be more than enough to track down the woman he's looking for. All he has to do is come up with a plan, carry it out and get what he wants. That's the next step. For example: Andrés could go in, looking around him with a scatty, hesitant expression on his face.

"Good morning," he could say, smiling shyly and going over to the young woman at the till.

"Good morning."

"I have a bit of a problem." Initially, Andrés would linger over the pauses, then gabble furiously, trying to confuse the woman. He would heap her with words and endless stories, creating an overwhelming sense of confusion. "And all I have is this," he would say at last, showing her the half ticket. "Could you possibly help me?"

Or he could enter the shop, go straight up to the woman and propose a bribe. Or else, frankly, without further ado, with no twee preambles, he could adopt a straightforward approach and pour out his troubles, tell her all about his father's secret affair and the enigma of the woman's voice that has brought him to this place smelling of lavender and steam. Whichever ploy he finally chose, Andrés emerged from the dry-cleaner's with a name, address and phone number. The woman is called Inés. Inés Pacheco.

One day, when he was a boy, he followed his father. He was fifteen at the time. Well, everyone has been fifteen once. He can't remember why he did it, there are no clues, no explanations. His memory offers him only a feeling, something resembling rancour, an aggressive, piercing pain. Andrés is crouched down in the shelter of the dusk, spying. He's hiding behind a truck being loaded up with crates of vegetables. There are carrots, celery, courgettes, and two crates full of red onions. In the crate at the back he can see only the green fingers of some leeks. His eyes take in this landscape, peer through the windscreen and finally reach the other side of the pavement. That's where his father is. He's talking to a couple of men. Andrés is a little disappointed. He has a fantasy about his father having a secret affair with another woman, who has at last replaced the memory of his mother.

He had waited patiently near the building where his father worked and then followed him, just like in the films, always keeping a few yards behind, occasionally changing pavements to avoid being seen. His father went to have a coffee with his usual friends, then made his way to that alleyway and those two men. He took some notes out of his wallet and offered them to the men. They exchanged glances. They didn't seem at all pleased. One of the men, the taller one, shook his head. The three of them talked briefly. Andrés was getting more and more tense. He was afraid something would happen. Suddenly, with no warning, one of the men punched his father in the stomach. A short, sharp blow. Javier Miranda doubled up, the breath knocked out of him. The other man, almost in the same movement, as if they were working in tandem, swiftly brought up his knee and struck Javier Miranda in the face. Andrés couldn't move. He didn't know what to do. He wanted to do too many things at once. He wanted to race over and punch those two men, he wanted to run away, he wanted to cry out, to call for help, he wished he'd never followed his father. The two men took his father's wallet and watch and walked quickly away. Andrés stayed where he was, stock still and frozen behind the truck, while his father struggled to his feet, moaning and wiping the blood from his mouth. Not even then did Andrés dare to go over and help him. His fear of giving himself away, of revealing that he'd been following him and why, was too strong. His father limped away. In his memory, Andrés' eyes are red. The memory smells of red onions.

That night, his father came home late. Andrés pretended to be asleep. The following morning, he told Andrés some silly story about tripping and colliding with a door in the office. That's how he explained the cuts to his eyebrow and mouth. They never talked about it again.

Nevertheless, Andrés remembers it now, on the fourth floor of a small building in the old part of Chacao. He's standing outside the door to apartment 4–C. He has just rung the bell.

After a few moments, he hears or thinks he hears the sound of footsteps. He could almost swear it's the sound of sandals approaching. The door opens gently and there she is. Or so Andrés thinks. She must be Inés. She's a woman of about sixty. She was obviously very beautiful once and still has all the elegance of a once-beautiful woman. She has very dark shiny hair. She looks at him without saying a word, she doesn't even seem surprised. She merely waits.

"Good afternoon, are you Inés Pacheco?"

"Yes," says the woman.

What follows is silence, because Andrés doesn't know how to continue. He's run out of script, he suddenly finds that he has no idea what to say, and is now hanging from the edge of this scene, afraid he might drop abruptly into the void. The woman is still looking at him, waiting, increasingly bewildered. Then after a pause, Andrés asks, perplexed:

"Don't you know me? Don't you know who I am?"

The woman studies him more closely, as if trying to locate Andrés' face in her memory.

"No," she says quite naturally.

"I'm Andrés, Javier Miranda's son."

Only then does the woman react, and she seems to tense slightly, as if something inside her had cracked. But she still says nothing and makes no move to invite him in. She remains silent, looking at him. Andrés merely watches expectantly.

"I think there's been some mistake," she says at last. Her tone of voice is warm, but she pronounces each word rather too exactly, too precisely. "I don't know who you're talking about."

And without letting Andrés add anything further, or giving him a chance to react, she gently closes the door. Andrés stands in silence for a few seconds, taken aback. Then he hears, or thinks he hears, the sound of sandals approaching and then moving off again.

The situation is getting worse all the time. Karina arrives at the office now at half past six in the morning, when the cleaners are just starting work, when the grime and the shadows are still part of the dawn itself. She leaves at eight o'clock in the evening, two hours after finishing her day's work. Dr Miranda has urged her to take a holiday too, but she refuses. She watches the time pass on the computer screen, always waiting for the unexpected to happen, for a new e-mail suddenly to appear.

"You're going mad," says Adelaida.

"Typhus is less contagious than hysteria," wrote Joseph Roth. Adelaida doesn't know these words; she has never read and never will read Joseph Roth, but this is more or less what she thinks too.

"Look at the state of you!" she cries. "Look at the state you're in over that guy. He's passed his sickness on to you!"

"It's your fault," says Karina in her own defence, albeit rather unconvincingly. "You were the one who persuaded me to start writing to him!"

"That has nothing to do with it. Don't try and put the blame on me. You're the one who let that madman poison you."

Is that the right word? Has she been poisoned? Karina herself wonders the same thing several times a day. It not only has to do with her response to Ernesto Durán's absence; there's something worse, something she hasn't even dared confess to Adelaida, something she may not even want to put into words.

It happened for the first time two Wednesdays ago. On her way home, Karina stopped at a video shop. She thought that perhaps a film would help her overcome the all too frequent

114

bouts of insomnia that had been troubling her lately. She went into the shop at seven o'clock at night, the place was packed, and she was afraid there wouldn't be any new films available. She went straight to the shelves marked "Comedy". Perhaps she just needed something to distract her, perhaps that would help her to sleep. However, as she advanced slowly down the narrow aisle, running her eyes over the titles of the films, she began to feel nervous, strangely nervous. It wasn't something she could describe clearly, but suddenly, the shop seemed much too small; suddenly, she felt hemmed in, unable to move freely, in need of air. A shudder ran through her. Almost a faint electric shock, like a distant nerve twingeing. The voices of the other customers appeared to come at her from varying distances and at different volumes, almost as if they were circling her or dancing, suspended from the shop's suffocating ceiling. She felt unsteady. Her left eyelid was twitching. As if it had a life of its own. As if it were independent. Her forehead felt cold and clammy too. Her saliva was like sand, difficult to swallow. She couldn't help thinking again of Ernesto Durán. She grabbed the video that was closest to hand and walked briskly over to the queue at the till.

There were three people ahead of her. Karina couldn't believe this was happening to her. She tried to calm herself, tried taking deep breaths, clenching her fists and digging her nails into the palms of her hands, as if pain might help her keep control. Inevitably, the same fear she had so often read about began to surface. Was she about to lose consciousness? She wasn't going to faint right there, was she? To conceal these feelings, she crouched down, pretending to check some detail on her shoes. This allowed her to rest one knee on the floor and to feel safer, steadier, more balanced. This wasn't her idea. She'd read about it in a letter. Ernesto Durán had told her of something similar happening to him when he was queuing up at the bank. The other customers, of course, haven't heard that story. Women don't usually keep bending down to check their shoes while they're waiting in a queue. Karina was aware of this, but couldn't help it. Whenever she got up again, she would give a stiff smile, make some gesture, some pointless attempt at explanation. Then she was almost immediately overwhelmed by a terrible feeling of fragility. She was sweating profusely. She felt as if she were hyperventilating, as if a strange weakness were invading her being, as if she could no longer stand the lack of oxygen. There was now only one person ahead of her in the queue. Being able to look outside, through the glass door, was the one thing that gave her a tiny bit of peace, but even that was not enough. Then came a burning sensation, a fierce pricking in her throat. Karina started to scratch her neck. She was afraid it might be an allergy, although she couldn't help connecting it with the unrelenting feeling of asphyxia. She swayed back and forth on the spot; she stretched out her arms, tried to expand her lungs, took deep breaths through her nose and mouth, rested her hand on the shelf containing sweets to one side of the counter, bent down, checked her shoe again, and straightened up, wiped the sweat from her cheek with one hand, glanced out of the corner of her eye to see if the other people behind her in the queue were looking at her. Then she could stand it no longer. She plonked the film down on top of some chocolate bars and raced out of the shop. Gasping for air, she only got as far as the steps leading out of the small shopping centre. She sat down, not caring now or even thinking about the people hurrying past her, their legs almost brushing her.

She doesn't know how long she sat there. She can only

remember feeling that she had been saved. Only just in time, at the very last second. Was this what Ernesto Durán experienced? Was this how he felt? Had she caught it from him, did she suffer the same sickness?

Andrés is studying the results from the latest C.T. scan. He's brought them home with him and is sitting on the bed, holding the image up to the light coming in from the window so that he can view his father's brain. The bluish sheet reveals the spots with a clarity he now finds unbearable. Mystery always helps to make death a little more bearable. All this scientific exactitude is intolerable. What's the point of it? Who does it help?

Suddenly his hand feels heavy, he finds it hard to keep holding that picture aloft. How many of these has he seen before? Too many. How often has he been faced with definitive images like these? He lost count long ago. After a while, you only count the ones you save, the exceptions. The dead go into a separate account, they keep their own tally. Perhaps he's remembering that novel by Louis Ferdinand Céline, in which a doctor "described illness as he would describe the face of an old acquaintance". That is what weighs on Andrés now. His long, long relationship with illness. Perhaps he has seen too many people die.

Once he dreamed that all his dead patients got together, that they were members of some kind of club: Dr Andrés Miranda's lost patients. He doesn't like that word "lost". It seems unfair. Perhaps because he knows that, sooner or later, doctors always lose. They are never going to have a good average. Defeat is their destiny. In that dream, his patients looked as ill as when he knew them, as if time had frozen them in that particular passage of their life. They were all very pale, or, rather, grey, but they were all almost exactly as he remembers them. Don Agustín Mejías was stumbling along, dragging with him a stand from which hung a saline drip. Señora Arreaza was in a wheelchair. Tomás Hernández still had a bandage round his head. Silvina Rossini was wearing a printed scarf over her bald head and was coughing loudly. Old Pimentel was lying naked on a stretcher, eyes glazed and lips parched. They all looked just as they had the last time he had seen them. His unconscious mind had gone no further, but had simply made do with the first images it came across. In the dream, none of his patients were looking at him. They were just walking about. Occasionally, they would exchange brief greetings, but they never turned round to see him; they acted as if he didn't exist. "The next time I have this dream," thinks Andrés, "my father might be in it. Perhaps he'll pass me by too, without noticing me, without looking."

Mariana finds him lying on the bed, alongside the scan results. It's five o'clock on a Saturday afternoon.

"Are you alright?"

Andrés doesn't answer. His eyes are closed, but he's obviously not asleep. Mariana goes over to him, sits down beside him, runs her fingers through his hair and gently scratches his scalp.

"Come on, let's go to the cinema with the kids," she says.

Andrés emits a low groan, then slowly shakes his head.

"You've pretty much ignored them for three weeks now. They know you're looking after Grandpa, but they still need you. They miss you," she adds, placing a slight emphasis on the last three words.

Andrés opens his eyes.

When his father and Mariana first met, Mariana was naked.

Andrés and Mariana had been going out together for a month. Taking advantage of a weekend when his father had gone off with some friends to Barquisimeto, Andrés had invited her over to spend the night at the apartment. They cooked seafood risotto – the squid was hard and chewy and they'd used too much saffron – drank white wine and made love into the small hours. On Sunday morning, they took a shower together. There they were, under the shower, arms around each other, kissing, when they heard the front door open.

"Andrés," called his father. "Are you home?"

It was eleven in the morning. The sound of water bouncing off the tiles filled the whole apartment, as if thousands of needles were hurling themselves to their deaths on the floor. Mariana instinctively sought shelter in his arms. Andrés tried to wrap the plastic shower curtain around them, meanwhile frantically thinking what to do next. He didn't have much time. His father was already in the bathroom.

"Didn't you hear me?"

"Yes, yes, of course. I just wasn't expecting you." Andrés tried to sound natural, pressing Mariana to him. "I thought you weren't due home until tonight?"

"Oh, the whole thing was a disaster. The axle shaft on the car we were travelling in broke before we even got as far as Chivacoa. We wasted the whole afternoon getting it fixed and had to spend the night in Urachiche. That's why we came home this morning."

Then Mariana and Andrés heard the familiar sound of pee falling into the toilet bowl. His father was standing right next to them, peeing. Andrés imagined him pointing his penis at the water; Mariana inadvertently let out a nervous giggle. It was a strange sound, like an elongated squeak, a stifled exclamation.

Andrés gave her a warning squeeze, but it was too late. Surprised and concerned, his father pulled back the shower curtain. He stared in astonishment at the sight of a completely naked Mariana clinging to Andrés' body.

"Hi, Dad," Andrés said, making an attempt at a smile.

His father left the apartment and didn't come back for two hours. He returned bearing a pizza and behaved as if the scene in the bathroom had never taken place. Even when Andrés tried to talk about it, he quickly changed the subject. Two weeks later, when Andrés introduced him formally to Mariana, his father held out his hand and said hello with just a hint of mischief in his eyes. And that was that.

"What are you thinking about?" asks Mariana.

Andrés didn't reply at once. For some time now, he's had the feeling that his memory has become part of a new privacy, of a space he can't share. He even remembers things differently, in more detail, storing up different sensations; he feels that the past has become too lively a corpse.

"What are you thinking about?" Mariana asks again.

"About Inés Pacheco," he says.

It's true that she does still occupy his thoughts. Or perhaps she's simply part of that past of which he knew nothing, a past that was lost and now suddenly appears in this emphatic, obsessive way. Señora Pacheco has taken up residence in his mind. She lives there now. Several days have passed and his father still hasn't said anything to him about her. He can't understand why. He assumed she would tell his father, that she would have phoned him up at once: "Your son has just come to see me. You might have warned me." Why, then, has his father said nothing? Why did he never mention this woman? Why does he still keep her hidden away, why does he hide this part of his life? Andrés cannot help but feel hurt. This is hardly the moment for him to be feeling that his father is a stranger too.

"Perhaps they don't see each other any more," says Mariana. "Perhaps they're not even friends," she adds after a pause. "Perhaps they even hate each other."

"You're forgetting that she phoned his apartment just two weeks ago. I answered her call," Andrés counters.

"You think it was her, but you don't actually know that for sure. You're playing the detective, but you could be wrong. The woman who phoned your father wasn't necessarily Inés Pacheco."

"O.K.," agrees Andrés, "you're right, but Inés Pacheco does exist. And something went on between her and my father."

"Is that what bothers you?"

"No, of course not."

"Like I said some days ago, everyone has a private life. Even your father."

Andrés suddenly picks up the image of his father's brain and shows it to his wife.

"What the hell is this, then, Mariana? Isn't *this* someone's private life?"

She looks at him slightly reproachfully and tensely. Andrés calms down and bows his head. She leaves the room, saying that she'll go to the cinema with the kids on her own. Andrés falls back on the bed again. For the first time, it occurs to him that the illness might take away from himself and his father something he had never thought it would: conversation, the ability to talk to each other. The illness is destroying their words as well.

*

The pact between Javier Miranda and Merny also includes going together to the workshop. Merny accepts it as another of her duties, as another contribution to the bus ticket that will save her son. They always go in the mornings, behind Andrés' back. Javier Miranda found out about it from a nurse.

"The workshop has helped a lot of people," she told him.

At first, he wasn't interested, but after the third session of chemotherapy, he asked the nurse for more information. Now here they are, for the first time. Merny seems uncomfortable and keeps looking uneasily about her. He seems almost distracted, as if he'd ended up there by mistake. They're in a large room on the ground floor, where a couple of dozen plastic chairs are arranged in a circle. There's also a small table with a pile of papers on it and a thermos of coffee. A very pleasant lady welcomed them and took their enrolment money. When told that companions were not allowed, Javier paid for Merny to enrol as well. The other participants look as glum as he and Merny do. A kind of lukewarm sadness seems to circulate amongst them. There's one lady with a zimmer frame, a very thin, pale young man, another man with only one leg, a woman who keeps rubbing her hands together and staring at the floor? I wonder how I seem to them? thinks Javier Miranda. What will they make of me? Merny is asking her own questions. Will one look tell them she's the servant, the help? Or will someone assume she's Javier Miranda's partner? Or will they think there's no connection between them at all, and that she's there because she's ill too, because she, too, needs to negotiate with death?

"Good morning. My name's Roger Picón Heredia and I want to welcome you all to the first session of this new workshop."

He's a tall, dark, well-built man, although he moves with great agility, as if he weighed nothing. He doesn't have to try very hard to make people like him. He has a natural charm and a brilliant smile. While he talks, he walks among the participants, looking at each person and smiling at them.

"Before we start," he says, "I want you all to get rid of those resigned expressions, as if you'd been forced to come here, as if this were a club for the sad and the hopeless. Well, it's not. On the contrary. Make no mistake, this workshop may be called 'Learning to die', but it's not an undertaker's. We come here to learn and to value how wonderful our life has been and still is. That's why you're here. Because you still want to squeeze a bit more out of your life and to celebrate it. O.K., everyone on their feet. That's right, everyone. We're all going to stand up. Now hold hands. That's it. Ready? O.K."

At this point, Merny wishes she had waited outside in the street. Now she's hand-in-hand with old Señor Miranda and the very thin, very pale young man. The young man's hand is sweating. The old man's hand is cold. It suddenly occurs to her that the young man might have some terrible, contagious disease. She immediately lets go of his hand. The young man looks at her, and Merny, embarrassed, takes his hand again.

"How are you feeling?" The leader of the group walks slowly past them all. He stops next to Merny. "Are you feeling nervous?"

"A bit," she whispers awkwardly.

"Don't worry. Nothing bad is going to happen."

Then he moves on. Merny feels a slight pressure on her right hand. She assumes it was an involuntary movement, but then Javier Miranda's hand sends her another signal, another brief squeeze. She looks at him. He's smiling mischievously at her, as if the whole situation were highly amusing, as if he were a child in need of someone to share the joke with.

"Now close your eyes. Breathe deeply. That's it. One, two. One, two. And again. Very gently. Excellent. Now I want you to go on a journey into your memory and visit all those marvellous places and marvellous moments you've known. Moments of love, joy, triumph. With your loved ones, with your family, with your friends. Keep your eyes closed and experience those moments again. Keep breathing deeply. One, two. And now, say with me: I'm alive."

The group finds it hard to get in the mood. They shoot sidelong glances at each other, uncertain what to do. They don't so much follow the facilitator's instructions as trail reluctantly after them.

"No, not like that. No-one's going to believe you if you say it like that. Come on, loudly: I'm alive!" The man moves round the circle, touching them, patting them on the back, encouraging them. "Come on! I'm alive!" He reaches Javier Miranda, puts his arm around him and says: "Come on, maestro! Louder. I'm alive!"

Until, finally, they manage to form an enthusiastic, or at least reasonably enthusiastic, chorus. Merny is reminded of the evangelical Christians who live in her barrio. They shout too. They hold hands and shout. And sing. They don't smoke or drink, which is good, but the women aren't allowed to wear trousers. And that's bad. Merny feels the very thin, very pale young man's hand growing sweatier.

"Now say with me. I'm alive. And my life has been good. When I think about my life, about what I am, only one word comes into my mind: thank you. Yes. Thank you. Because my life is a miracle. Because my life is a gift. Thank you. Thank you, life."

They all rhythmically repeat the same words. Then they sit

for a few seconds in silence. They're all waiting for the facilitator to say something, to tell them what to do next. They don't dare open their eyes. Javier Miranda starts to think that the workshop is a bit of a con, a small circus for those wounded in combat, for those who cannot return to the battlefield. And so they're offered several sessions with this determinedly cheerful preacher, intent on convincing them that you can also be joyful in defeat.

"Right, you can open your eyes now," the man says at last.

And he again welcomes them back with a smile. He asks them all how they feel. He makes them see that they're feeling better, that this exercise has given them a new glow, that their initial mood of despondency has lifted. Then he makes them all say their name out loud. Just their name. Merny is terrified. She's never done anything like this before. She's never had to tell so many people her name. When her turn comes, she hesitates, she almost feels as if the word will lose its way in her throat, that when she tries to say it, her name will run away, will get lost inside her body. Then she discovers that it's all much easier than she thought. She says "Merny". Out loud. And then she experiences a sense of relief. And pride. Yes, when she says her name and finds that nothing terrible happens, that she's alright, that her name is just as much a name as anyone else's, Merny feels pride, a strange peace, the satisfaction of having passed a test.

"Why are we here? Each of you has a very personal reason for being here. It may be that the reason is a cause of shame or sadness to you. You feel weak, vulnerable. You're afraid. Do you know what? You're not alone. No, you're not the only ones. Look around. There are men and women here, young and old. There are white people, brown people, black people. We none of us look very alike. You probably didn't even know each other until today. And yet I'm sure that at the moment you're all experiencing more or less the same emotions. And I'm going to tell you something. A lot of people wouldn't even dare come to this workshop. I mean it. Even the name frightens them. People just like you, who feel the same, but who have allowed themselves to become frozen, who have closed the door on their life and given up. But you haven't, you've taken the risk, you did it, you're here, at the first session of a workshop called 'Learning to die'. That's why I'm applauding. I'm applauding you. I mean it. Because I'm really excited to see you here. Because you're amazing and I congratulate you."

They take the bus back to the apartment. Javier Miranda doesn't want to go on the metro. He prefers to be above ground so that he can see the city. It's midday, the sky is intensely blue and clear and the sun, high up, is like a white stone. They manage to get a seat and sit down next to each other. Merny says nothing. She only speaks when he asks:

"So what did you think of it?"

"Odd."

"In a good way or a bad way?"

"I don't know, just odd."

He looks at her and smiles. And she smiles too.

She doesn't even re-read the e-mails now, she knows them by heart. She has read them so often that she might even be able to recite them. She doesn't need to look at them. At some point, a transition, a journey took place, and the words of Ernesto Durán stopped being something outside her, on the computer screen or printed on a piece of paper, and became something that lives and breathes inside her. She has even found herself counting adjectives. There are so few. More than once, she has been surprised by the memory of a particular phrase, for example: "There was a ravine inside my body." Karina takes a worryingly short time to mentally locate that sentence in the first few lines of the fifth paragraph of the third letter sent by Durán on 12 June at 6.24 in the evening.

She hears a report on the radio about people who are setting up a strange society, the National Patients' Union. They want to form a kind of trade union where people can defend themselves against doctors, protect themselves from medicine. It immediately occurs to Karina that Ernesto Durán is likely to be involved, that he's probably one of the leaders of this infant organisation. She tries to listen as closely as possible to the item. That same night, on television, she sees an interview with some of the people behind the movement. The first to speak is a lady who describes how she was bitten on the arm by some strange creature, which she assumed was an insect, although she didn't know which kind. It wasn't any common-or-garden variety, not a mosquito or a gnat or a midge. It was something else, she says. Anyway, her arm started to swell up and turn purple and she had no option but to go to the A. & E. department. She was seen by the doctor on duty, who – according to her – merely poked around in her inflamed arm with a syringe. He didn't ask her anything, or say anything, or give any explanations. Karina guesses that the woman is telling the truth because, even now, when she recalls the moment, she grows angry and finds it hard to get the words out, she seems about to weep with rage. When the doctor finally grew tired of scraping around beneath her skin, he said that he'd found nothing, left her under observation for two hours and then gave her an antibiotic, explaining that the antibiotic wasn't for the bite, but for what he'd been doing with that wretched syringe. "Don't worry about the bite," the doctor said. "It's nothing. It'll clear up in time." She paid a small fortune and went home with an idea jumping about inside her head: a National Patients' Union.

Then several other people speak. A boy whose little sister died from a lack of oxygen in a hospital in the west of the city. A man with only one leg, who accuses an anaesthetist of negligence. A nurse who claims to know the world of doctors from the inside and who says that, as well as being a nurse, she, too, is in need of nursing. There's no sign of Ernesto Durán. Karina even tries to get in touch with the organisation, and manages to speak to one of the people interviewed, but to no avail. No-one knows him, no-one knows anything about Durán.

"You're not well. This obsession of yours isn't normal."

Adelaida thinks someone has put the evil eye on Karina, that someone – who knows, perhaps Ernesto Durán himself – has paid for some kind of spell to be put on her and send her mad. She also believes that Karina should fight back with the same medicine. Through herbs, a medium, voodoo, or a soothsayer, some power that doesn't belong to the known world, that calls for more faith than science. Karina has given her a vague, truncated version of what's happening to her. She hasn't again experienced quite what she did in the video store, although there have been a couple of similar incidents, the worst of which happened only two days ago, on the metro. It was, of course, the rush hour. Karina was standing, crammed up against the other passengers. It took only two seconds for her to realise she was about to have an attack. She was gasping for air, her heart was pounding, she broke out in a cold, sticky sweat, her tongue swelled up so much she felt as if she had a huge toad in her mouth, a rough-skinned creature scraping against the roof of her mouth and preventing her from breathing, suffocating her. She jumped out at the next station, swearing that she would never again travel in the metro.

Adelaida insists that it isn't something physical or biological. No syringe can protect you against the evil eye. No antibiotics can do battle with a curse. Faced by such a situation, science crumbles, it's a war that has to be waged by different means, with different weapons. Karina prefers to think that it's just a phase, part of the temporary anxiety she's feeling, that it won't last, that she'll wake up one morning and it will be gone, that somewhere a pleasant, calm Thursday awaits her, with no fear, no feelings of asphyxia, no dizziness, a Thursday when Ernesto Durán will not even be a memory.

He spent the morning in the operating theatre. Although he chose to work in general medicine because he'd never felt at ease with surgical practice, Andrés does sometimes help out at the occasional operation. Usually, this is at the request of a friend. Miguel often asks him. Today it was Maricruz Fernández. They had opened up a patient with two tumours on her liver. Maricruz wanted Andrés to have a look at them, to get his opinion. The second tumour, in particular, was causing confusion. Half of it was soft and the other half hard, and only one side of it was cerebroid in appearance. This time, Andrés felt dizzy, something that had never happened to him before. As he bent over the woman's body, he suddenly felt as if the ground had slid from under him, as if he might drown in those intestines, plunge in and be lost for ever inside that dark, slimy liver.

He made an excuse and left as quickly as he could. He went to the cafeteria and drank a glass of orange juice. Now he's sitting outside the door of the chemotherapy room, staring into space, thinking. In the last week, his father has deteriorated terribly fast. The voracity of certain diseases is truly repugnant. Andrés finds his tolerance for such things is decreasing as his own suffering increases. He even finds the clinical terms unbearable:

> neoplasy exeresis staphylococcal empyema
> pleural empyema anastomosis iliocolostomy
> biopsy haemostasis prosthesis laparotomy
> ischemia lithiasis

These are words that travel up and down hospital corridors all the time. He closes his eyes and he can hear them. They glitter and gleam in the middle of any conversation, they stand out among the other simple words, the words that serve only to live, but not to confront death. It seems to Andrés now that they form part of a pretentious, useless dictionary. This morning, when he went to fetch his father, he found him sitting on the bed, naked. He looked unconscious, although his eyes were open. Andrés hesitated for a few seconds, thinking that his father might feel embarrassed. Such unexpected intimacy was very cruel. He decided to go over and sit down beside him. His father didn't move. From closer to, Andrés could see how fragile he was. His spindly legs. His limp penis, like a finger fallen asleep in the wrong place, as if it had never been a penis. His bones were more prominent. They now provided the dominant framework of his body. The expression on his face was one of deep disillusion.

"How are you?" Andrés put his arm around his father's shoulder, taking care to feign a quite incomprehensible optimism.

"Terrible." His father still didn't look at him. "I've had enough,

130

Andrés. I don't want to go on. I don't want any more treatment."

"You've just woken up feeling a bit low, that's all," Andrés insisted, although the words felt rough on his tongue. It seemed to him it was his duty, his role, to say something of the sort.

"I woke up today feeling exactly as I did yesterday. And the day before yesterday. And the day before that."

"Come on, I'll help you get dressed."

"No, I mean it. I don't want to go."

"You have to." Andrés crouched down in front of him. They looked hard into each other's eyes.

"It hurts," his father said after a pause, almost in a whisper. Almost like an exhalation. "Everything hurts. It hurts like hell."

Now, sitting in the corridor, he can no longer hear the clinical words, no more *neoplasy ischemia pleural empyema*. It hurts like hell. That's all he can hear.

Julio Ramón Ribeyro wrote in his diary: "Physical pain is the great regulator of our passions and ambitions. Its presence immediately neutralises all other desires apart from the desire for the pain to go away. This life that we reject because it seems to us boring, unfair, mediocre or absurd suddenly seems priceless: we accept it as it is, with all its defects, as long as it doesn't present itself to us in its vilest form – pain."

Andrés decides to spend the rest of the day with his father. He invites him to have lunch in his favourite restaurant, a discreet place whose food has been much praised, assuring him that they make real home-made fare. His father doesn't seem very keen. Andrés insists. So much so that, in the end, it's as if his father were making a real sacrifice in accepting. They don't enjoy the food. His father is feeling horribly nauseous. He has such chronic acid reflux that he can't eat anything. They go home in silence. His father undresses and gets into bed. Andrés sits down beside him again. What can he do? What does his father expect of him? Is there anything he can do, is there any way of helping him? His father lies down on his back, staring vacantly up at the ceiling. Andrés opens the drawer of the bedside table.

"I was looking for your pills the other day and I came across this," he says, and shows him the book.

His father doesn't seem particularly interested, and so Andrés holds the book in front of his eyes. His father eventually manages to whisper:

"A nurse at the hospital recommended it to me."

"*Dying with Dignity*," Andrés reads. "Not exactly optimistic."

"Life isn't optimistic."

Andrés sighs, leans closer and affectionately strokes his father's bald head.

"You're not thinking of doing anything foolish, are you, Dad?"

"The only foolish thing I can do is to die, and I'm doing that right now."

Andrés doesn't know what else to say. He drops the book onto the bed and continues stroking his father's head. They both stay like that for a few moments, until Andrés decides to take a risk.

"Why did you never tell me?"

"About what?"

"About Inés Pacheco."

His father sits up and looks at him. He seems more disappointed, even angry, than surprised. Despite his weak state, he maintains a haughty, almost severe mien.

"I met her. I went to see her," says Andrés.

And then the old man slowly deflates, as if that sudden burst of spirit had simply emptied out through some secret hole. He gives a snort and slumps back onto the bed. Then he closes his eyes, as if he didn't want to hear any more.

"Didn't she tell you? Didn't she mention it?"

His father remains sunk in his own thoughts.

"Does she know what's happening to you, that you're ill?" Andrés continues asking questions even though his father refuses to answer.

After a few moments of silence, Andrés also lets himself slide very slowly onto the bed, so that he's lying beside his father. Then he, too, lies staring up at the ceiling. They probably both just wish it would end, that it was over. Death is preferable to pain. Illness is a very bitter toll to pay, a tax so capricious that it can make death the object of all our final desires.

"I smell bad," his father says suddenly, still with his eyes closed.

He's right, but Andrés doesn't respond. Every illness produces inside the body its own particular distinguishing marks.

"It's as if I'd already started to rot."

Andrés doesn't look at him either. He doesn't dare.

"It's just that you're very depressed, Dad," he whispers, a lump in his throat.

"Can't *you* smell it? I smell strange, of ammonia and things. Even when I've showered, I still smell."

Andrés gently reaches out and takes his father's hand in his. He closes his eyes, as if he wanted to close his memory too, as if he didn't want it to hold on to that image.

"I'm desperate," he confesses. "There's nothing I can do. I don't know what to do."

The silence is a knife plunging into the skin of the afternoon.

Neither of them dares now to open his eyes.

"What can a man do when, suddenly, one morning, he's told that he has only three or four weeks left to live?"

This is how the second workshop session begins. Two new participants have joined them: a very fat woman who has difficulty breathing, and a young man of about thirty, who looks healthy enough, but is clearly feeling uneasy and nervous. Roger, the same smiling facilitator from the first session, quickly gets the group involved.

"Think about yourselves for a moment. There may be people among us today who are in a similar situation. It wouldn't be the first time, I can assure you. I've led a lot of these workshops and there's often someone who has had just such an experience. But, if not, it doesn't matter. Just take a moment to do this mental exercise. Imagine that, at this very moment, a celebrated doctor, a notable specialist comes to you and says: sir, madam, miss, young man, I regret to inform you that you have only one month to live. What would you do?"

Merny thinks of Javier Miranda. She thinks of his age, of the pain he's in, of his terrible pallor. He seems to grow daily more absent. What has *he* done with these final days of his existence? Has he used them well or has he wasted them? Who can say? Who can judge?

"Obviously, it's not easy." Roger again walks round the circle. "We don't always react the way we think or believe we'll react. Perhaps, after receiving a piece of news like that, we might waste a whole week simply digesting, believing and accepting it. The big difference between human beings and other animals is that we're the only ones who know we're going to die. A dog doesn't know. A cat has no idea, cannot even imagine such a thing. On the other hand, we can. And we spend our lives thinking about it. Suffering and enduring that knowledge. More than that, there are people who spend their whole lives trying to avoid what they know, trying not to think about it. There are people who can only live when they forget they're going to die. That's why I'm asking everyone to do this exercise. Right, you've got four weeks left to live. What do you want to do with that time?"

When Javier Miranda found out the truth, he spent quite a long while trying to grapple with that question. He thought about his son, he thought about Mariana and his grandchildren, he thought about a long-dreamed-of trip to the Amazon, he thought, too, about Inés Pacheco. But he and Inés had long ago made a pact. Moreover, the idea of setting up a series of goals before he died became mixed up with the clear sense that, gradually and unstoppably, his death would become something ever more public. That is another of the consequences of being ill: the private agony becomes a collective ceremony. The result of this was that Javier Miranda began, instead, to want to withdraw, to hide away, to become more distant, more absent. As the days passed and the tests and treatments and doses of medicine increased, so any pleasure or delight he might feel diminished. This wasn't a selective deterioration. At that point, everything was lost. There are no half-measures when one says goodbye.

"What about taking a trip somewhere. That's a possibility. That's a great idea." Roger moves from one to another of the participants, searching out and sharing answers. "So where would you like to go?"

"New York," murmurs an old lady.

"New York, very good." He moves on, and finds himself in front of the very thin, very pale young man. "And what about you, Rodolfo, what would you do?"

"If I was told I only had four weeks left to live, I'd do everything I could to find a cure, to live longer."

"What for example?"

"I'd go and see one of those doctors who cure by laying their hands on you, I'd try natural medicine, I'd pray to María Lionza, I'd eat roots, I'd do whatever they told me to."

"Very good. Thank you, Rodolfo," he says, as he moves on, keeping a close watch on each member of the group. "Who else would like to say something?" He stops next to a man in his sixties, with a bandage over his eyes. "Ah, Don Esteban. What about you? What would you do?"

"I'd have it away with a Chinese woman," he says and roars with laughter.

Some of the other members of the group laugh too, others keep silent and exchange glances that presage future days of tittle-tattle.

"Well, I've never been with a Chinese woman. I mean it."

"I don't doubt it, Don Esteban. We believe you. That's perfectly fine." He stops suddenly in front of Merny. He bends towards her, resting his hands on his knees. His tone is warmer. "And what does Merny have to say? What would you do?"

Merny feels awkward. The whole group is looking at her and that frightens her. She feels as if she had done something wrong, or is about to. She's embarrassed. She feels that what she has to say is wrong, stupid, irrelevant.

"So, Merny, you have four weeks left to live. What are you going to do with that time?"

"Take my son to Mérida," she blurts out nervously, not even daring to look up.

*

"Dr Miranda!"

Karina is the first to hear him. Or so, at least, she thinks. Dr Miranda, who is walking by her side, appears not to react, but walks on as if he'd heard nothing, absorbed in his own thoughts. So much so that even Karina wonders if she really did hear it or perhaps imagined it. Then she thinks that's impossible, you don't imagine noises.

"Dr Miranda!"

She hears it a second time and feels the same shiver run through her. The voice comes from behind, from behind and from the left, from above too. Behind, above and to the left. Karina feels those two words crowd into her head. She had gone with Dr Miranda to help him carry some samples and, there they are, walking back to the office, strolling serenely down the corridor, when that voice appears, a voice that is like a bolt of lightning to Karina, but to which Dr Miranda appears oblivious.

"I think someone's calling you," Karina says at last, placing one hand on Dr Miranda's arm.

And then they both turn round. They do so quite naturally and slowly, although Karina experiences this quite differently, more quickly and more tensely. She's quite right: Ernesto is coming towards them. He looks so unchanged, so normal, that, for a second, Karina feels slightly disappointed. He doesn't even look thinner or paler, there's nothing to show that he has just been through a health crisis or a time of terrible suffering. Not that he's exactly in festive mood either, he approaches wearing a tentative smile and looking quite calm, timid but quite calm.

"Could I speak to you for a moment?" he asks, and his voice is neither cold nor hot, but he looks straight into Dr Miranda's eyes.

"The fact is . . ."

137

"It will only take a minute. Please."

Karina is beside herself with nerves. She doesn't dare look at either for them for very long. She lowers her eyes and lets her gaze wander from her shoes to Dr Miranda's shoes, elegant in brown leather, and from there to Ernesto Durán's shoes, also leather, but older and cheaper, and black with no laces and with rather pointed toes.

Only when she feels the doctor's hand on her shoulder does she realise that she has drifted off, escaped from the moment. She looks up, and when she becomes aware of Durán's eyes on her, she immediately feels a wave of heat inside her. She hopes she doesn't blush. She hopes she doesn't do anything. She tries to appear as normal as possible.

"Can you go on ahead and give these results to Dr Sananes?"

She says she will, of course, naturally, she nods, takes the pieces of paper, again says, yes, of course, drops the papers, again says yes, while all three of them bend down to pick up the wretched results. She feels closer to the shoes now. And it seems to her absurd to think such a thing. It bothers her, irritates her. Almost as much as it does to find herself in this ridiculous situation. As she moves off, her pulse is ahead of her, beating much faster than she can walk. When she turns a corner in the corridor, she stops to catch her breath, to try and calm herself, to think. She peers round the corner and watches the two men in the distance. Ernesto Durán is wearing blue trousers and a white cotton shirt. He's the one doing the talking. He is making small gestures with his hands. What on earth can he be saying? Karina senses that it will all end in disaster. The idea that everything will finally be revealed, the fear of being discovered, weighs on her far more than knowing that Ernesto Durán is alive and well. What will happen now?

In Chekhov's story "Ward 6", the doctor says to the patient: "There is neither morality nor logic in my being a doctor and your being a mental patient, there is nothing more to it than idle chance." Perhaps Karina is thinking something not dissimilar as she watches them. Perhaps she even believes that she is the "idle chance" that has brought these two men together as doctor and patient. Shouldn't she go over and explain everything to them right now? Shouldn't she go and tell them that she alone is the hinge that allows them to look at each other and share in the same movement? But Karina is paralysed, frozen. She cannot even breathe very deeply. She stands there, stunned, watching Durán and Miranda. This only lasts a moment though.

What's going on? As soon as they're alone, Ernesto Durán makes a brief gesture in the air as if he were giving a turn to an invisible screw. He attempts a smile too.

"Thank you," he says.

And then he looks at the doctor and gives him a knowing nod. Andrés Miranda just stares at him, perplexed, still waiting.

"It's been a long time, eh?" Durán adds, after a pause.

Andrés is growing more bewildered by the minute. Durán finds this attitude rather intimidating. Or so it would seem. He was apparently expecting something else, some other reaction. He had probably imagined this meeting quite differently.

"If you say so."

Ernesto Durán nods more energetically this time, like someone obliged to get to the point and to stop beating about the bush. He clears his throat, then looks straight into Andrés' eyes:

"The illness, doctor," he says gravely. "It's killing me."

Andrés feels that something inside him is deflating. He suddenly has no idea what he's doing here with this man he doesn't know. There must be some mistake, some terrible mistake, this morning, in the middle of a hospital corridor, some ghastly error, some absurd misunderstanding. Andrés looks behind him, looks around, instinctively repeating the gestures of someone who feels he has been mistaken for someone else.

"I'm serious . . ."

Serious? He's serious. The illness is killing him. For a moment, Andrés considers brushing him off with a curt response, for example: "Well, it's the same for us all, isn't it?" Yes, he could say something like that, then just turn and leave. He could also slap him on the back and cheer him up a little: "Don't be so solemn about it, it's not so bad. That's why we live, in order to get ill." He would accompany him a little way down the corridor and then escape to his office. Another possibility would be to talk to him about his father. To show him the latest test results. To say to this stranger what he finds so hard to say to his own father. To tell him that he's terrified. That he doesn't know how to get through the next moment. That he can't imagine himself alone, so alone, when Javier Miranda is no longer Javier Miranda, when he no longer exists. The illness is killing us.

"I'm sorry," he says at last, trying to control his voice as he speaks. "I think there's been some mistake. I don't know why you're telling me this."

The man then moves his head twice from side to side, as if he had water in his ears.

"Don't you recognise me, Andrés?" he asks suddenly, looking at him hard and addressing him by his first name.

"No, I'm sorry, but I don't think we've even met."

"I'm Ernesto Durán."

Andrés Miranda moistens his lips with his tongue. For a few seconds, he seems to be thinking hard. Ernesto follows with his eyes that imaginary journey, that invisible search.

"I'm sorry," Andrés says again after a pause.

Then he makes a gesture intended to bring the conversation to a close.

"Wait." Ernesto stops him. He squeezes his arm hard. "The letters."

"What letters?" Andrés asks in bewilderment.

"The e-mails we've written to each other."

"I'm sorry, but now I know you're mistaken."

"But . . ."

"I don't use e-mail. I don't think I've ever replied to an e-mail in my life. You're mistaking me for someone else. If you look in the directory, you'll see that there's a gastroenterologist who has a surname similar to mine, perhaps that's what happened."

And before Ernesto can say or do anything else, Andrés has walked off, hurriedly, without turning round, without even saying goodbye, as if the meeting had been a slip, a blunder, to be dismissed with cordial excuses, in the middle of a hospital corridor.

When Mariana sees the three drops of blood on the floor, she realises the moment has come. She's known for days now that this is a symptom that could appear at any time. It's not *a* symptom but *the* symptom, the one they've all been expecting. She immediately regrets that it should have happened on a Wednesday, at four in the afternoon, when her father-in-law has come to spend a few hours with his grandchildren in their apartment. Andrés has gone out. Relations between them grow sourer every day; he's permanently in the blackest of moods, which Mariana can understand, but she simply can't bear it any more. She, too, wishes it would just end once and for all.

The three drops form a little triangle on the floor. Mariana looks at them and then goes in search of more drops, until she finds a longer trail, a route.

"Javier!" she calls.

She goes along the corridor towards the room where the children are slaughtering small galactic monsters on the T.V. screen.

"Children!" she shouts. "Is Grandpa with you?"

She walks on, her head bent lower to the floor. She bumps into a small table. Something falls off.

"Javier! Children!"

Finally, ashen-faced, she reaches the room: the volume on the T.V. is deafening. Her children are alone. Without asking or saying anything, Mariana immediately turns and hurries to the bathroom, where she knocks twice on the door.

"Grandpa!" she says, still trying to appear calm.

No answer. She sighs, hesitates, looks at the floor. Another blood stain. She doesn't knock this time, she grips the handle and pushes. The door won't open. It bumps against the unconscious body of Javier Miranda. Mariana pushes harder, crying now and desperate. One of her children says something to her as he comes down the corridor.

"Don't come near. Go away!"

The boy freezes. Mariana tries to slip a hand through the crack and push her father-in-law's body out of the way.

"Phone your dad!" screams Mariana. "Phone your dad! Now!"

Andrés has turned off his mobile phone and, still undecided, is once more standing outside Inés Pacheco's apartment. Overwhelmed as he is by a sense of powerlessness, he feels that perhaps this is something he can do for his father: although he does not know her, this woman is his father's other love, the one other experience of love that's left to him. Why isn't she with him now of all times? Why isn't she there for him? Why will neither of them talk to him? Andrés thinks that perhaps this is a gift he could give his father: a visit from Inés Pacheco. But all he has is that vague presentiment. He rings the bell.

After a matter of moments, he again hears that shadowy whisper and then the door opens. It's her. However, this time, when she sees him, she immediately tenses up. She looks uncomfortable and stares at him with a kind of impotent melancholy.

"Why have you come back?" she asks.

"Forgive me," Andrés says, feeling nervous and awkward. "May I come in?"

"No," says the woman, glancing behind her and leaning against the doorframe.

"It's important."

Andrés looks at her almost pleadingly. Her discomfort grows. But she says nothing.

"He's very ill," Andrés explains. "My father is dying."

The woman takes in a great gulp of air, lowers her head, and when she raises it again, her eyes are bright with tears.

"Did you know?"

She doesn't answer. She just gazes at him in utter desperation. Andrés doesn't know how to contain his own anxiety. He wishes he could simply spirit her away. Then, just when she seems about to say something, a voice comes from inside.

"Inés."

A tall, grey-haired man appears; he's rather frail-looking, but has a pleasant, kindly face.

"Who is it?" he asks, joining them at the door.

"This young man is looking for . . ." Inés stops, uncertain how to continue. "He's looking for someone." Then she, with a particularly emphatic gesture, explains: "This is my husband."

The man remains at her side, studying Andrés with curious eyes. He smiles politely.

"Who are you looking for?"

"Oh, no-one," stammers Andrés. "I was given the wrong information. I'm so sorry. But thank you, thank you very much," he says.

"That's alright."

The door closes almost noiselessly. The voices of the man and the woman linger on the other side. The man asks something. The woman answers. Then all is silence.

When Andrés turns on his mobile phone again, all he hears is a howl. The ambulance siren is already opening up a wound of sound in the late afternoon.

Dear Ernesto,

How can I begin to explain everything that I have to explain to you now? Where to begin? I had better begin with my name: Karina Sánchez. I'm Dr Andrés Miranda's secretary. I don't know if you remember me, we've met occasionally at the consulting room, and we've spoken on the phone as well. We only ever talked about appointments, as part of my work, nothing else. And yet, although you may not believe it, we know each other far better than that, we have had much closer dealings.

Let me explain: among the tasks Dr Miranda assigned to me is that of dealing with any correspondence sent to his e-mail address, which he uses to receive social

144

invitations, promotional material from pharmaceutical companies, and as a place to divert messages from certain patients, patients like you. Forgive my frankness, but when I decided to write to you this morning, I was determined to be completely honest with you, to tell you the whole truth, whatever the cost to myself.

Your first letter came to this address. I read it, told the doctor about it and he gave me instructions not to reply. When the second letter arrived, I said nothing. I assumed that the order he had given still held, no matter how many e-mails you sent. However, when I read your e-mail saying that you were following the doctor, I felt frightened. It seemed to me that things were getting serious, even dangerous. That was when, on the bad advice of a friend, I decided to reply to your letters myself.

Now in the midst of your surprise and indignation, you may find it hard to understand why I did that. I ask myself the same question all the time. At first, I thought it would be an innocent, amusing game, but gradually came to realise that I was wrong. You may not believe me, but I swear that it was you and what you said, the sincerity with which you wrote, that revealed to me the monstrous nature of what I was doing. I know my actions are unforgivable, because I now feel that what I did wasn't just an error, it was a crime. I stole the doctor's identity, I passed myself off as him, and, worst of all, I deceived you, I used and abused your privacy without your permission.

I can assure you that I will quite understand if, from now on, you hate and despise me. It will be painful to me, but I know that you would be absolutely within your rights to do so and I will try to accept it. I have no excuses.

I must confess one other thing. You changed my life, Señor Durán. I now understand perfectly what you feel, I know what it is to feel as you do, to experience those same symptoms. In some way you infected me. You and your words. And so, when you stopped writing, I began to grow anxious, to feel worse and worse. I'm not saying this to flatter you or to excuse my errors. I'm saying it because it's true.

In the hope that this finds you well and that you will, one day, feel able to forgive me, I remain,

Yours sincerely,

Karina Sánchez

He's in room 508. The A. & E. department treated him and cleaned him up, but decided there was no point in sending him to intensive care. There wasn't much more they could do. He was weak and in terrible pain. They've put him on a saline drip. They're keeping an eye on his blood pressure and his pulse. He's been given morphine.

Mariana is outside in the corridor with the kids. Andrés has just arrived. He goes over to the bed and looks at his father. He's rapidly becoming just a bony structure, as if his skin were also slowly bidding farewell and clinging to the bone; as if the clear outline of the skeleton were rising to the surface. Andrés bends over and kisses him on the forehead. His father opens his eyes. They look at each other and exchange sadly knowing smiles: there's no need for any fuss, they both know perfectly well what's happening.

"What a shame I was at your apartment," murmurs Javier. "I hope the kids weren't upset."

"Don't worry. If it had been at your place, you would have been all alone."

Javier Miranda thinks about this for a second. He tries to speak, but it's very hard. Everything is getting harder and harder, everything is an effort.

"You shouldn't have let Merny take all that time off to go to Mérida."

"It was a deal we made," he murmurs.

Andrés nods. His father closes his eyes again. He's breathing with difficulty. Andrés looks for something to do: he checks the flow of saline solution, checks the information on the medical records left on the bedside table. None of those facts and figures mean much now. Every patient writes his own history. The stories told by illnesses each follow a different order, a different rhythm. They never repeat themselves, even though all have the same ending.

Andrés goes back to his father's side. He takes his pulse, places his other hand on his forehead. The cold is edging nearer. Andrés wishes he could lie down beside him as he had before, embrace him and weep. His father again tries to say something, but can't; he opens his mouth, clears his throat, attempts a sound and can manage only silence; his tongue is dry; the words he can no longer speak, that he no longer has, hurt him.

"Don't try to speak," Andrés says. "Don't say anything."

He feels tears burning beneath his eyelids. They sting. He doesn't know what to do. He once more places his hand on his father's forehead. Suddenly they look at each other. Andrés sees that his father is quietly crying too. He kisses him again and squeezes his hand.

"Everything changed," Andrés sobs. "Ever since I told you that you were ill. Ever since we knew."

His father shakes his head, as if to stop him speaking. Andrés won't be silenced.

"No, it's true, we both changed. We didn't know how to handle it. We got angry, it freaked us out . . . We should have talked more – I don't know – tried to have a better time together."

His father looks at him and smiles fondly. He swallows hard and makes as if to touch his son's face, but that feeble gesture quickly fades. Andrés wipes the tears from his father's cheek.

"This isn't something you can rehearse for," his father murmurs, jokingly, as if trying to make light of the situation. "No-one told us it would be like this."

Three floors up, in the office, Karina is still phoning relatives and friends, as Mariana had asked her to do. Call the people closest to him and explain the situation. The inevitable has happened. She has done this, feeling rather awkward and nervous. She doesn't quite know how to explain. What can she say? That the inevitable has happened and they should come quickly because his life is nearly at an end? Just as she's about to make another call, a little icon appears on her screen: a new e-mail has arrived in her in-box. She immediately puts the phone down and turns to the computer. She feels even more excited when she sees the name of the sender: Ernesto Durán.

Dear Dr Miranda,

I hesitated for a long time before writing to you again. I finally decided that I would and I'm going to explain why. I haven't heard from you for a while now. The last time I wrote, I was in the middle of a crisis, I asked you for help and you failed me. You never phoned. I was in urgent need of help, and you didn't come.

It wasn't easy. It took me weeks to recover, but fortunately my body slowly pulled itself together and, eventually, my condition stabilised. All this has had its consequences, of course. Among other things, let me just say that I lost my job. Gradually, though, I'm returning to normality. I can't deny that, at first, I felt very bitter towards you. I determined that I wouldn't write to you again. And I didn't. I never again sent you an e-mail. I didn't follow you either. I didn't come to the hospital looking for you. I wanted to erase you from my life, Doctor.

"Has he finally replied?" Adelaida is standing in the doorway, watching her. "I know your face, Karina. It's from him, isn't it?"

Karina nods, rather put out by the interruption.

"So what does he say?"

"It isn't for me. It's for Dr Miranda."

"I don't believe you," exclaims Adelaida, coming to peer at the screen over Karina's shoulder.

But I couldn't do it, Doctor. Every day, I woke up with the same feeling of emptiness in my hands, as if something was missing. I went to bed with the same anxiety. This wasn't just a repetition of my old symptoms, it was something else, something much deeper. Then, this morning when I woke up, I saw everything so clearly. I need to write to you, Doctor. Even though you've let me down, even though you don't read my letters, despite all that, I need to write to you.

If you answer me, that's fine. If you don't, it doesn't

matter. But writing is the one thing that makes me feel better, the only thing I really need. Before, I always thought that one wrote for other people, for the other person to read what one had written. Now I'm not so sure.

"The guy's mad!" mutters Adelaida. "Doesn't he say anything about that time he came to see the doctor? Or about the letter you wrote him? Doesn't he say anything about that?"

"Exactly," says Karina.

"What do you mean 'exactly'?" Adelaida stares at her in bewilderment. "Don't you see? That's his only sickness."

Karina nods, a strange, glad smile on her lips. And tapping lightly on the keyboard, she begins writing her response.

In the corridor on floor five, outside room 508, Mariana and her children are waiting in silence. Inside, Andrés, for how long he doesn't know, has been sitting bent over his father, an uncomfortable position, but it's the only way he can get close to him. Everything is so ephemeral. They are the only solid thing in that room. When he hears his father cough, he sits up. They look at each other again.

"What do you want? What can I do for you?"

His father thinks for a moment.

"Talk to me," he says with some difficulty, as if he had to drag the words to his lips. "Talk to me about us."

Silence is a sharp stake. Andrés feels as if his tongue were a stone in his mouth. Then he realises that this is all they have, the one shared thing that remains to them: their last words. That hoarse, weak voice signals the end of the body, sound is the only bit of life they still have.

What are last words like? What do they taste of?

His father makes a small gesture, again reaches out his hand, as if to draw him closer, to have his son still nearer. Andrés bends forward, almost crouched over him now.

"This is how I want to go," murmurs his father. "Listening to you talking."

And he again closes his eyes. Perhaps even opening and closing his eyes hurts him now. Passing the time hurts too.

Andrés feels as if his mouth were full of tree bark. He feels a deep, deep sadness. He's crying, not holding back now, not trying to stop his tears. His father's hand between his two hands feels ever lighter. Why do we find it so hard to accept that life is pure chance?

His father opens his eyes again, tries to smile, and gives him instead a look of fragile tenderness.

"Talk to me," he says again. "Don't let me die in silence."

The translator would like to thank Alberto Barrera Tyszka for all his help, and, as always, Annella McDermott and Ben Sherriff.